## Praise for *The Light Jar*

"A thoughtful and hugely empathetic book: a consolation for readers who, for whatever reason, might be feeling a little out of place in the world." —*The Guardian*

"Tense and threaded with mystery . . . Thompson adeptly draws the storylines into a cohesive whole that rewards readers with a satisfyingly hard-won resolution." —*Booklist*

"This is the kind of book that will matter most to kids facing loss and family disruption themselves, letting them know that imagination is a useful tool for developing courage in difficult times and that sometimes you need to go back in time in order to move forward." —*Bulletin of the Center for Children's Books*

"Carefully and beautifully written. Strongly recommended." —*School Library Journal*

## Praise for *The Goldfish Boy*

★ "This empathetic debut is a middle-grade whodunit with a very special heart." —*Kirkus Reviews*, starred review

"A multilayered mystery at once suspenseful and heartrending." —*Booklist*

"A compelling story with a hearty dose of mystery and adventure." —*School Library Journal*

"Both a genuine mystery and an emotionally charged examination of fear and loneliness, this is a terrific read with warmly engaging characters." —*Daily Mail*

"A genuinely clever mystery." —Robin Stevens, author of the Murder Most Unladylike series

# LISA THOMPSON

# THE LIGHT JAR

SCHOLASTIC INC.

Copyright © 2019 by Lisa Thompson

First published in the United Kingdom in 2018 by
Scholastic UK Ltd., Euston House, 24 Eversholt Street,
London NW1 1DB.

All rights reserved. Published by Scholastic Inc.,
*Publishers since 1920.* SCHOLASTIC and associated logos are
trademarks and/or registered trademarks of Scholastic Inc.

The publisher does not have any control over and does not
assume any responsibility for author or third-party websites or
their content.

No part of this publication may be reproduced, stored in a
retrieval system, or transmitted in any form or by any means,
electronic, mechanical, photocopying, recording, or otherwise,
without written permission of the publisher. For information
regarding permission, write to Scholastic Inc., Attention:
Permissions Department, 557 Broadway, New York, NY 10012.

This book is a work of fiction. Names, characters, places, and
incidents are either the product of the author's imagination or
are used fictitiously, and any resemblance to actual persons,
living or dead, business establishments, events, or locales is
entirely coincidental.

ISBN 978-1-338-21631-8

10 9 8 7 6 5 4 3 2 1    20 21 22 23 24
Printed in the U.S.A.    40

This edition first printing 2020

Book design by Chris Stengel

*For Stuart, Ben, and Isobel*

# CHAPTER 1

# THE NONHOLIDAY

I love Mum's tunnel-singing trick.

She always did it when she drove us to Grandma's for one of her Sunday lunches. In the car, Mum would put the radio on and we'd both sing along to whatever was playing, although I'd usually have to make up the words. We had to go through a long gray tunnel on the way there, and when we drove into it, the music would go all crackly and fizzy and then disappear altogether. I'd stop singing, but Mum would just keep going. I'd watch her from the back seat as she lifted her chin and shook her head to make the high notes go wobbly. The tunnel would go on and on and on, but Mum wouldn't stop and then . . . *whoosh*, we'd come out into the daylight, the radio would come back on, and Mum would be singing in *exactly* the right place. I'd clap and she'd laugh.

She hadn't done it on this journey yet, even though we'd already been through a long tunnel. The radio was on, but this time Mum wasn't singing. She was too busy looking into her rearview mirror every few seconds at the dark road behind us.

"Why are we leaving now?" I said. "Couldn't we have waited until the morning?"

Mum switched the windshield wipers on, and they creaked slowly across the glass as if they'd just been woken up too.

"We want to beat the rush hour, don't we?"

She looked at me in the rearview mirror and her eyes crinkled like she was giving me a big smile, but I wasn't sure as I couldn't see what the rest of her face was doing. She was acting like we were going on holiday, but it was pretty obvious we weren't. First, we only had two small bags and my backpack with us, and you need far more than that for a holiday. And second, I'd only known we were going away when she shook me awake at one in the morning saying we had to leave right now. This definitely wasn't like any holiday I'd ever been on. She'd stood by the window, watching the street while I quickly packed a few things, still half-asleep. I knew she was looking out for Gary even though he was away on a business trip and not due back until the next morning. We went downstairs in the dark, and Mum put our bags into the trunk of a car that was parked outside. I'd spotted it near our house when I'd come home from school. There was a sticker in the back window advertising a rental company, and I'd guessed it belonged to one of our neighbors. Mum didn't have her car anymore. Gary told her they didn't need two cars after he moved in.

I gave a big yawn as I looked out the window on to the wet road. The clock on the radio said 2:55 a.m. Nearly three in the morning. I don't think I've ever been awake at three in the morning in my whole life. I was awake at two once, on a New Year's Eve. We weren't at a party or anything; someone let fireworks off in a field near our house. I'd been dreaming I was in World War II and I had crawled into a metal trash can to escape the bombs, and when I woke I realized the bombs were actually fireworks.

The highway was deserted at 2.55 a.m. We hadn't seen another car in ages.

The rain began to drum really hard on the car roof like a billion fingertips all going *rat-a-tat-tat*. This went on for about ten minutes and then suddenly it stopped. It was just like someone had turned off the world's biggest hose. At first I thought it was some kind of weird weather like I've read about in the best book ever, *Freaky Things to Freak You Out*, but then I saw brick walls and orange lights and I knew we were just going through another tunnel. I looked at Mum and wondered if she was doing her tunnel-singing trick in her head.

I've read *Freaky Things to Freak You Out* three times now. Apparently, there is a ninety-six-year-old man in Brazil who has a pet maggot living in his eyelid. Mum says it's all made up and they've just written those stories to fool kids like me, but there's a photo of him holding the maggot, so it must be true. I brought the book with me and planned to start at the beginning and read the whole thing again. As well as *Freaky Things to Freak You Out*, I'd packed:

My soccer ball alarm clock (you can't actually kick it, it's just round)

A blue flashlight

A tennis ball

A puzzle book

Two pens

Mrs. Ellie-Fant (a stuffed toy that I've had since I was a baby)

My Ask Me a Question magic ball.

I got the magic ball out of the front pocket of my backpack and pressed the ON button. The little screen glowed green as the words scrolled across . . .

**Greetings from the Ask Me a Question Magic Ball!**

**Think of a thing and answer my questions . . .**

**. . . then be amazed as I read your mind!**

You can conjure up anything and, as long as you answer everything correctly, it reckons it can tell you what you are thinking. Sometimes it gets it right if you pick something easy like an apple or a train or a balloon, but most of the time it's pretty rubbish.

In my head I thought of a clown. I pressed the START button and it began:

**Is it a vegetable?**

*No.*

**Does it come in a box?**

*No.*

**Can you buy it in a supermarket?**

*No.*

I wasn't saying the answers out loud; I actually had to press a YES or NO button.

**Does it walk on two legs?**

*Yes.*

Can you see it?

*Yes.*

Is it used for entertainment?

(I thought about this one. I didn't find clowns particularly entertaining, but I guessed it was a yes.)

*Yes.*

It asked me loads more random questions, and then the little green words on the screen got faster:

You cannot fool the Ask Me a Question Magic Ball . . .

I've got it!

I am the smartest being in the whole land!

Be amazed when I tell you this . . .

. . . I can actually read your mind!

This goes on a bit too much if you ask me. It's just showing off about how clever it is, and it takes ages before it gives you an answer.

Are you thinking of . . .

. . . an imaginary friend?

Useless.

I huffed, switched it off, and put it back in my bag.

A lady on the radio was giving a weather forecast with warnings of icy conditions and sleet, with heavy snow to come later in the week.

I'd been putting off asking Mum too many questions. She'd looked so anxious and on edge before we left, but now I could see her shoulders relax.

"Where are we going, Mum?" I said.

"Oh, you're going to love it!" she said, her voice sounding all weird and squeaky. "It's a sweet cottage that belonged to one of Grandma's old friends: a gardener named William. There are two bedrooms, an old wood stove that heats up the whole place, and a little garden with a door that goes through to a forest. William died a few months back. There's no one around for miles, so it's a real secret haven. We went there for a holiday once when you were small. Do you remember? He let us stay in the house while he was away visiting friends."

I thought about the holidays we'd had with Dad when he still lived with us. We went to Spain once, and me and Dad went on a paddleboat five times. That was a brilliant holiday. I also remembered going camping—it rained a lot, but I remember it was funny because I couldn't get out of my sleeping bag. The zipper had gotten stuck, so Mum had to pull me out of the top. I couldn't remember visiting this cottage, however much I tried.

The inside of the car lit up. Someone behind us had their headlights on at full beam. It was the first car I'd seen for ages, and I looked around to see who was out in the middle of the night like we were.

"Keep your head down, Nate," Mum said, squinting in the mirror. The other car was getting really close and the lights dazzled my eyes, so I scrunched them up to try to see.

"Nate, did you hear me? I said get down!"

I slid down in my seat. Mum kept looking in her mirrors, first the one on the side and then the one in the middle. She was looking in her mirrors more than she was looking at the road in front of us.

The car overtook us, and Mum slowed down as it passed and put her hand up to her forehead as if she was scratching it. The car drove in front of us for a while, and then its orange light blinked and it turned off to the left, and Mum's shoulders sank once more. Her hand appeared around the side of her seat, and she patted me on the knee.

"Sorry I shouted. I just couldn't see out of the mirror properly, that's all," she said.

We sat in silence for a bit, and I looked at the streetlights reflected in the puddles on the road. It reminded me of something from when I was little, but I couldn't quite place what it was. It was the color I remembered. A yellowish, glowing color. I suddenly felt like I wanted to cry.

"Mum?" I asked. "Are we really going on vacation?"

Mum rubbed the side of her face with her hand and took a deep breath before she answered quietly.

"Not exactly, Nate."

# CHAPTER 2

# THE COTTAGE

"Why can't we stay with Grandma?" I asked Mum.

We sat in the car as the rain hammered down and stared at the dirty gray cottage that was lit up by Mum's headlights. The image I'd pictured of a holiday we'd once had in a cozy, quaint cottage completely vanished. About thirty years ago this house was probably quite pretty, with its white walls and roses around the door. Now the walls were the color of a muddy puddle, and it looked like it was slowly being swallowed by blankets of thick, dark ivy. I didn't recognize this place at all. The dirt track that we turned down from the main road must have been at least two kilometers long. Mum was right: This was really off the radar.

I didn't want to go inside. I wanted us to turn around right now and go somewhere else.

"I thought it might be a bit untidy . . . but this?" said Mum, and she leaned forward and rested her chin on the steering wheel. "This is terrible! How has it been left to get in such a state?"

"We should go, Mum. I don't like it here. Let's go to Grandma's."

She ignored me again. Mum and Grandma had had a big argument and hadn't spoken since Granddad's funeral, which was months ago now.

"Wait here, Nate, and I'll go and find the key. This weather is probably making it look worse than it is. I bet it's not so bad inside."

She pulled her cardigan tightly around her neck, then got out into the torrential rain and waded through the weeds to the front door. She ran her hand along one edge of the porch roof and then went around to the other side, out of sight.

I stared through one of the cottage windows. There was a faint yellow light coming from the corner of a room. The car window steamed up and I rubbed at it with my sleeve and squinted into the gloom, but the glow was gone. I must have imagined it.

Mum appeared holding a large key in her hand. She tugged at the ivy on the porch and then fumbled with the lock and began to push at the door with her shoulder. She had to keep stopping to wipe the rain out of her eyes, but after ten more shoves the door began to inch open and she squeezed through, tugging at it from the inside before beckoning me to join her.

I stared up at the ramshackle old house. Rainwater poured from a hole in the gutter above one of the windows, which made it look like it was crying. Mum waved me toward her again. She was splattered with mud and her hair was plastered to her face and she was gripping the side of the door as if it was helping to hold her up.

"I don't want to be here," I said under my breath, and then I picked up my backpack and opened the car door.

---

Mum flicked a light switch in the living room and a bare bulb dangling in the middle of the ceiling spluttered to life, giving off a feeble glow.

"Look, Nate. We have light!" said Mum, but I didn't answer. She made her way back to the front door.

"You wait here and I'll get our bags."

I wanted to run after her, shut the stupid, awkward door, and get straight back into the car. The house looked like it hadn't been cleaned for about a hundred years, and there was a smell like something was rotting. In front of the stone-cold wood stove was a sofa that was probably quite squishy and comfortable fifty years ago, but now it looked like it had had its insides sucked out. Something moved in the gloom and I jumped. Sitting on one of the arms of the sofa was a scruffy brown chicken. She cocked her head at me, and blinked with a dark, round eye.

"What are *you* doing here?" yelled Mum, walking in and waving our two bags wildly. "Get out! Go on. Shoo! This isn't your home!"

The chicken gave a squawk and then did a half-hearted flutter up onto the windowsill and jumped through a square of broken glass. She huddled outside on the ledge, sheltering from the freezing rain as much as she could.

The sofa was covered in lots of gray lumps, and it was only when I stepped closer that I realized it was chicken poo, which probably explained the smell.

"We can't stay here, Mum. Look at the sofa, it's disgusting."

Mum didn't turn around. She just stood in front of the broken window, staring at the bird.

"There are droppings everywhere. And there are probably rats and all sorts of things crawling around. And we haven't even been upstairs yet. Where are we going to sleep? We can't stay here— we've *got* to go somewhere else!"

The chicken sank her head into her body as far as she could, her eyes barely open as the rain and wind blew, ruffling her feathers. Mum's fingers were clenched by her sides. She didn't turn around.

"Mum? I said we've got to go! Let's just get in the car and drive to Grandma's, okay?"

She was saying something quietly to herself. Her eyes were wide and fixed on the chicken and she was shivering, her clothes soaked through.

"She just wanted a home, Nate. She didn't mean to make a mess. She just wanted a little home to shelter in."

Tears were running down her face, but she wasn't making any crying noises. I put my arm around her and patted her hand.

"It's okay, Mum. It's just a chicken."

I looked out into the night, at the pounding rain and the silhouettes of dark trees.

"I don't know what I'm doing, Nate. I don't know what's right or wrong any more," said Mum, her voice shaking. "You know that feeling when you think the ground is going to split in two and you could just fall and keep on falling forever? Like Alice does when she tumbles through that rabbit hole into Wonderland? But rather than floating down and landing at the bottom you just keep on going. Down and down and down."

I shook my head as she looked at me. I didn't know the feeling she was talking about. I was scared. I hadn't seen her like this before. It was as though her body was there, but her insides were missing, just like the sofa. She blinked and her eyes seemed to come back into focus again and she quickly wiped her wet cheeks and patted me on the arm.

"I'm just tired, Nate, that's all."

She peeled off her wet cardigan and hung it over an old wooden chair.

I held tightly to my backpack at my shoulder. I didn't want to go back, but I didn't want to stay here either. Mum headed toward a doorway that must lead to the kitchen.

"I'm going to see what I can find to patch the hole in the window. Why don't you go on upstairs and see how the beds look? We'll both feel better after some sleep, I'm sure."

She turned away and I stood there for a moment, thinking about what to do. Then I headed back through the living room door and stood at the bottom of the stairs. I pressed the light switch and the bulb at the top flickered. It looked very dark up there. I took a deep breath and held on to the banister. Each step groaned as I walked, but amazingly, I managed to get upstairs without crashing through to the floor. At the top of the stairs was a bathroom with an old-fashioned toilet with a chain that you had to pull to flush. There was a fat spider sitting in the middle of the bathtub, and I tapped the side and watched as it scurried away down the drain.

The next room had a double bed covered with a patchwork quilt, a small wardrobe, and a large, old chest of drawers next to a window. It didn't look too bad at all and would be perfect for Mum.

The other bedroom was darker, with a small, low, square window and a wardrobe in one corner. There was a lamp on a cabinet, and I switched it on. On the bed was a brown quilt that had a picture of a cowboy on horseback twirling a lasso in the air. I vaguely remembered sleeping in a bed like that before. The image reminded me of something in my *Freaky Things to Freak You Out* book. I sat down, unzipped my bag, and took it out. The book was divided into four parts:

*Seriously Silly Science!*

*It's a Crazy, Crazy World!*

*The Peculiar Past!*

*Animals Are Bonkers!*

I flipped to the *Peculiar Past* section until I found the page I wanted.

*On a dark night in 1882, cowboy Angus "Big Shot" Roach had an AWESOME ENCOUNTER when he spotted a mysterious spacecraft close to his campfire . . .*

*"I ain't never seen anything like it in my whole life,"* Angus reported. *"I thought an alien was gonna come down and suck my brains right out!"*

*Yee-haw to that, readers!*

Under the text there was a cartoon of Angus sitting by a blazing fire as a green flying saucer hovered nearby. The cowboy's mouth dangled wide and his eyes bulged with shock.

I jumped as Mum appeared in the doorway.

"You're not reading that silly book again, are you? You do know it's all made up?"

I quickly closed the covers. "No, it's not."

"It is! Tell me one thing in that book that is actually true."

I quickly flipped to page thirty-seven and read out loud. "If you mouth the word *colorful*, it actually looks like you are saying 'I love you.' Try it on a friend right now!"

I looked at Mum and she smiled and folded her arms.

"So, what am I saying now, Mum?"

I silently mouthed the word *colorful*.

Mum laughed.

"I love you too, Nate."

I slammed the book shut. "See?! I told you! I was saying 'colorful,' not 'I love you.' This book *isn't* lies. It's just stuff we've never heard about before. That doesn't mean it isn't true!"

"All right, Nathaniel, calm down. There's no need to get so angry with me."

I sat on the bed and stuffed the book back into my bag. I hated it when she called me Nathaniel.

"I don't like it here. I want to go to Grandma's," I said, not looking at her. I heard her sigh heavily.

"Listen. I'm just doing what's best for us, Nate. That's all."

"Best for us? How is it best for us to be here? It's horrible!"

I threw myself down on the bed and turned my back on her, waiting for her to leave. After a moment or so I heard the floorboards creaking as she went back downstairs. I sat up and got my Ask Me a Question magic ball out of my bag.

**You cannot fool me . . .**

**. . . I will guess your word after a few, simple questions!**

**Go ahead and try my magical powers.**

I pressed START.

**Does it live in the sea?**

*No.*

**Does it have four or more legs?**

*No.*

**Can it be scary?**

*Yes.*

I carried on answering the questions until the ball got to its show-offy bit.

**Be amazed when you see I can read your mind . . .**

**. . . you cannot fool the Magic Ball!**

**Is your word . . .**

. . . a monster?

I threw the ball onto the floor, and it rolled underneath the bed.

I'd been thinking of Gary.

———————————————

I lay down on the cowboy bed in the stinky, dirty cottage and listened to Mum moving things around in the living room. It sounded like she was trying to clean up a bit, but just half an hour later I heard the stairs creak as she made her way to the top. I expected her to come in to check on me, but after the toilet flushed I heard the other bedroom door squeak open. I waited for a bit and then I got up and went out onto the landing. Mum was lying on top of the bed with her eyes shut.

"Mum? Are you okay?" I asked, and I sat down on the corner of the bed.

"I'm fine, Nate. I just need to sleep, that's all." She patted my hand, and then she pulled it to her face and kissed it.

"We're safe now, darling. He can't find us here."

# CHAPTER 3

# OPERATION: CLEANUP

It was ten o'clock the next morning when I woke up. The winter sun streamed through the brown curtains, and I could hear Mum singing. I got out of bed and made my way down the creaky stairs.

The cottage looked a little brighter in daylight, but it was still very dirty. Mum had tried cleaning the chicken poo off the sofa, and the patchwork quilt that had been on her bed had been thrown over the top. The smell was still there though, and the rest of the room looked pretty dreadful. The carpet was covered with a thick layer of gray dust, dog hairs, and a few feathers. There were drapes of cobwebs fluttering in every corner, and along the mantelpiece over the wood stove was an assortment of figurines, pots, and vases, all covered in a thick layer of grime. In the center of the mantelpiece was an old clock that had stopped at eleven o'clock.

I took a look outside. Mum had put a square of cardboard over the hole in the corner of the window to stop the chicken, or anything else, from getting in. The garden was just a jungle of weeds all clambering over each other for breath.

"Morning, Nate! Well, you certainly look a whole lot better after some sleep. Isn't it lovely and quiet here? I slept like a baby."

Mum appeared in the kitchen doorway. She was wearing jeans and a stripy blue-and-white sweater. Her hair was tied up in a ponytail at the top of her head, and she had a big smile on her face. I hadn't seen her looking this happy in ages.

"Morning. What have we got for breakfast? I'm starving."

Mum grinned. "Come and have a look," she said, and I followed her into the kitchen. "You know our little friend on the sofa last night? I found a clutch of her eggs behind a cushion."

She held out a plate of yellow scrambled eggs that steamed warmly into my face.

"I thought we could eat and then get to work on cleaning this place a bit. What do you think?"

"Good plan, Mum," I said.

Cleaning up was hard work. The dog hair–covered carpet was, in fact, a large rug that we dragged out into the garden. I tripped and landed in a heap on top of it as Mum pulled me along, laughing. We managed to get it to a tree and drape it over a low branch.

"Right. Choose your weapon!" said Mum as she picked up two big sticks and held them out. I chose the smoothest one, and she grinned.

"Aha, good choice, my liege. That looks to be a mighty fine stick, does it not?"

I put on my serious face and nodded. Mum held her stick out to the side like a baseball bat.

"Okay. Are you ready for battle, Sir Nate?" she said.

"I am ready to do my duty," I said, trying not to laugh.

We counted together: "Three, two, one . . . Go!"

We hit at the rug with our sticks and clouds of dust appeared.

"Come on! You can do better than that!" Mum laughed and then began to jab at the rug as if she were in a sword fight with it. "En garde, you stinky, smelly carpet! Take that! And that! How dare you be so disgusting and horrible!"

I stopped hitting and watched Mum, laughing at her as she leapt about.

"Take that, you chicken flea–infested bundle of stench!"

I gave the rug a few pathetic pokes, but my stick kept bending.

"Come on, Sir Nate! Put your back into it!" said Mum. I pounded the rug again and again until there was a haze of yellow dust in the air all around us. After a few more beatings my hands were sore, and I stopped to catch my breath. That's when I noticed an iron gate set in the high redbrick wall at the back of the garden. Through the bars I could see the dark forest beyond.

"Where does that go?" I asked. Mum stopped hitting the rug and wiped her forehead, leaving a streak of dirt behind.

"That leads to the grounds of a big house. The man that owned this cottage, your grandma's friend William was the family's gardener, and many years ago he made up these little treasure hunts for the two children who lived in the house. When we stayed here on holiday we found an old one in the drawer and tried to solve it, the three of us. Do you remember? There was a chapel and a maze. It took us all over the grounds."

I thought about it for a bit. I remembered crossing a wide green lawn on Dad's shoulders. Mum had a piece of paper in her hand and she was laughing and running ahead saying, "This way! I think it's this way!" I don't think I really understood what we were doing, but it all seemed like good fun at the time.

"The poor family that lived there, well, they had a tragedy many years ago. It was very sad . . ."

She gazed off into the distance and didn't say any more.

I looked through the iron bars to see if I could spot the house, but all I could see were dark shadows everywhere.

"A tragedy? What happened?" I asked.

Mum pulled the rug off the branch.

"Someone passed away . . . Anyway, let's not talk about that right now. Let's get this back inside, shall we?"

We cleaned until late that afternoon, and then we both flopped onto the sofa and surveyed our hard work. Mum put her arm through mine. The cobwebs and layers of dust were gone, and the grime on the windows had been wiped away, letting in a bit more light. There was still a strong smell of chicken poo in the air, but it wasn't as bad as when we arrived, or maybe we were just getting used to it.

"I think we're going to like it here, Nate," said Mum, squeezing my arm. "Don't you?"

I suddenly thought about school. I would be walking home around now.

"Do you think anyone has reported us missing, Mum?"

She let go of my arm.

"Well, Gary certainly won't have called anyone, and I . . . I rang the school yesterday and said a relative had died and we had to go away for a few days. I thought it would give us a bit of a head start. So no. I don't think anyone will report us missing for a while yet."

We both sat in silence.

"I know you like it here, Mum, but shouldn't we go and stay with someone else? What if someone comes back and catches us? Can't we go and stay with one of your old friends?"

As Mum rubbed her forehead, I realized that since Gary had come along she'd fallen out with everyone. As far as I knew, none of her old friends had been in touch for months.

"Let's talk about that in a few days, shall we?" said Mum. "No one will be coming by here. For now, let's just enjoy being away from him. He will never find us as long as we keep quiet and we don't tell anyone that we are here. Okay?"

My heart fluttered against my chest like a trapped moth. I always got that feeling when I thought about Gary. Mum squeezed my hand and then jumped up.

"Right. I'm going to see if I can get this old wood stove going, and then I'm going to pop out to get some food."

"What? But you said we had to stay inside! You said no one could know we're here!"

Mum found a box of matches in a basket beside the stove, and she put a few lumps on the ash, crisscrossing some kindling on top.

"We've still got to eat, Nate. We passed a little supermarket about four miles away, so I'll go there and be back before you know it."

She peered into the wicker basket again.

"And while I'm at it I'll try to pick up some dry logs from somewhere. This isn't going to last us very long, and everything outside is too wet."

"I'll come with you," I said, getting up. I really didn't fancy being here on my own.

"No, you stay here and keep an eye on the fire. When it starts roaring just use the poker to slide the lever to the right. Okay? That'll keep it going and get the place nice and warm for when I get back. Don't open the stove door or touch anything without using the poker."

"But what if someone comes to the house? What if someone knocks? What if . . . What if Gary finds us?"

I paced up and down, and she stopped me with her hands on either side of my arms.

"He won't, Nate. You've seen how secluded this place is. Nobody knows we are here. And no one is going to turn up; it's been empty for a while. How about I get us a pizza and the biggest chocolate cake I can find? Does that sound okay?"

I nodded, but I wasn't happy about it.

She pulled on her boots and thick coat and wrapped her chunky pink scarf around her neck. It was getting dark outside and starting to sleet. She put her handbag on the table and took out a small plastic bag full of money. I don't think I'd ever seen that many bills in one place before. She usually used a card to pay for things, but I guess that Gary might be able to trace us if she did that. She must have been planning for us to run away and secretly saving cash. This thought felt very loud and sharp in my head. I didn't want to go back to Gary, but the thought of staying here scared me. I was about to say something when Mum spoke.

"Don't touch the fire, will you? Just do what I said when the flames really get going, and I'll put some more logs on when I get back."

I'd seen Grandma light her wood stove loads of times, so I had a good idea how they worked, but I was glad I didn't have to do anything apart from move the vent.

I followed her to the porch and watched as she pulled the stiff door open. The air was icy, and I could already see a thin white frost covering the car's windshield. Mum turned to face me.

"Remember, I won't be long, so just stay inside. We can't risk anyone finding us, you know that, don't you?"

I nodded. Her eyes looked like they were filling up with tears.

"It's fine, Mum."

She smiled. "I'm so sorry, Nate. I'm so sorry I've put you through this."

She gave me a quick kiss on the cheek, and then she mouthed something at me.

*I love you.*

I smirked and replied:

*I love you.*

She smiled. "Oh, I'm colorful, am I?"

And then she turned away and her breath escaped in small clouds as she hurried to the car. I stood watching as she slowly reversed the car and then turned left, back down the dirt track, the red taillights flickering behind the hedge until they disappeared altogether.

# CHAPTER 4
# THE TV GAME SHOW

The wood stove warmed the living room up really quickly, but there was a strong smell of soot. I turned on all the lights and then tried to draw the heavy curtains on the window that looked out onto the back garden and the dark, swaying trees, but they stuck on the rod. I looked up at the black sky, and just above the top of a bush I spotted a cluster of stars I recognized from my *Freaky Things* book. They were called the Pleiades and they were the closest star cluster to Earth, but they were still a very long way away. They twinkled at me in the cold night sky, and I felt myself shiver a little as I tugged on the curtains as hard as I could. I left the ones at the front open so that I would see Mum's car as soon as she got back.

The flames licked at the glass as if they wanted to get out, so I picked up the poker and slid the lever to the right, just like Mum had said. They instantly calmed down and crackled gently.

I hadn't eaten anything since the scrambled eggs, so I went to the kitchen to see what I could find. There was a box of crackers that had a best before date of five years ago, and some cans of food, including baked beans, peaches, and creamed rice. There was a half-eaten packet of mints that Mum had left, so I took two. I didn't fancy trying to work out how to use the can opener, plus

I didn't want to be too full for my pizza. As I walked back into the living room I saw a flash of yellow in the corner beside the wood stove. The fire was making the walls appear to flicker. That's what it must have been: just the flickering fire.

I wished there was a TV so I could put it on to keep me company. I'd look through the channels to see if there were any reruns of the best game show in the world: *How Well Do You Know Me?*

Mum and Dad had been contestants on that show before I was born, and we used to have a recording of it that we'd watch every Christmas. Mum would hide behind her hands as a younger version of her appeared on the screen, arm in arm with Dad as they skipped, laughing, toward the presenter, Barry Wonder, who was waiting with his microphone.

"Oh, Martin, look at my hair! What was I thinking having it so curly on live TV? I look like a sheep!" Mum would say, peeking through her fingers, hating and loving it at the same time.

Dad would be leaning forward with his elbows on his knees, transfixed.

"Look at me! Why didn't you tell me my shirt was so tight, Fiona? That's an all-inclusive honeymoon for you. I put on seven pounds during that holiday."

Dad would grin as Barry asked them about their wedding day.

"And what color did your bridesmaids wear, Fiona?"

My mum on the TV went all pink.

"They wore crimson, Barry, with an ivory sash."

The audience all went *ahhhhhhh* while I pretended to put my finger down my throat and vomit.

I loved it though.

I loved seeing them so happy.

They got through to the final round and were up against Stacey and Rob from Suffolk. But Stacey knew that Rob preferred strawberry jelly to black currant and Mum got Dad's choice wrong, so Stacey and Rob ended up with a car, a holiday, and two thousand pounds in spending money. As runners-up Mum and Dad got a golden statue of a bride and groom with a sash around them saying: "We Were Finalists on *How Well Do You Know Me?*" We kept that statue in our downstairs bathroom right up until Dad moved out, and then Mum gave it to a charity shop. I saw it in the window on my way home from school one day, and I went in and bought it for fifty pence. It was Mum and Dad's prize—no one else's. When I got home I hid it, wrapped up in an old school sweater at the bottom of my wardrobe. I wish I'd brought it with me now, in my backpack with my other things.

I stared at the space in the corner where a TV should have been and decided I'd probably feel a bit better if I had something to do. I counted to three, then sprinted to the hallway, up the stairs and into the cowboy bedroom, grabbed my backpack, and then went back down again. I put all the lights on as I went.

I took out Mrs. Ellie-Fant and tucked her under my arm. As

soon as Mum's headlights appeared I planned to stuff her back into my bag. I turned on the Ask Me a Question magic ball, answering all of its questions until:

I know what you're thinking . . .

I have used my powers of deduction . . .

The word you are thinking of . . .

. . . is . . .

. . . fire!

It was right for once. I clicked YES and the thing went into meltdown, flashing and dinging like it had solved the biggest problem in the world.

Next I tested out my blue flashlight—still working—and then I bounced the tennis ball continuously on the floor thirty-seven times until it hit a lump in the rug and rolled under the sofa. There was no way I was going to poke around under there, so I just left it.

I filled in a few word searches in my puzzle book, and then, on the inside of the back cover, I used my pen to create a tiny maze with lots of winding pathways.

Two hours had passed.

She should have been back ages ago.

I took another look out the window.

"Where is she?" I said out loud as I gazed into the cold night. I leaned on the windowsill and let my breath steam a big circle onto the glass, and then I used my finger to draw two people with smiling faces. Me and Mum.

I sat back down and turned to a fresh crossword in my puzzle book and started from the top.

**Across**

1. A bad dream (9 letters)

I clicked my pen and filled in the boxes.

*Nightmare*

# CHAPTER 5

# ALL ALONE

Mum had been gone for three hours.

I curled up on the sofa, feeling the warmth of the fire against my face. I was tired and my arms were aching from dragging the rug into the garden, but I didn't want to go to sleep in case Mum came back. I closed my eyes to rest them and imagined Mum stroking my hair, just like she used to do when I went to bed in the darkness back home. *"Don't worry, Nate. Just close your eyes and it'll soon be morning. I love you. Don't you forget how much I love you."*

The springs in the sofa dug into my side. Every now and then I opened my eyes and took a quick peek around the room. I'd left the light on, but the bulb was really dim and there were weird shadows on the walls from where the fire was reflected. I shut my eyes again.

I'd always hated the dark. But now I really, really hated it.

And my fear had gotten a whole lot worse after Gary came to live with us.

---

On the day he moved in, Mum had been really nervous. Nervous excitement, not nervous fear. She'd vacuumed the whole house twice and cleared out half of her closet so that Gary would have some space for his clothes. She'd also bought a new chest of drawers that was bigger than her old one so there was enough room for his things too. In the dining room, she'd put a big vase of flowers on the table, and there was a fish pie warming in the oven. Every time I went near her she pressed down on a tuft of hair that kept sticking up on the top of my head.

"Put some water on it, Nathaniel. It looks messy."

I'd met Gary loads of times, and he didn't seem like the kind of guy who'd be bothered about my hair, but I still went to the bathroom and did what she said.

It had taken me a while, but I liked Gary. At first I thought he would take up too much of my mum's time to leave anything for me, but he always included me when they went out for the day, and he brought me a present every time he came over. Once he turned up with a giant inflatable cactus. Mum had opened the front door and it was just sitting there on the step, swaying in the wind. When me and Mum stepped outside trying to work out where it had come from, Gary jumped out from behind the wall, shouting, "Surprise! This is just what you need in your room, Nate, don't you think? All boys need a giant cactus." Mum had laughed and he'd picked her up and spun her around, giving her a squelchy kiss on the lips. I left them to it and dragged the cactus inside and up the stairs, putting it in the corner of my room underneath the shelf with my jar of lights. It looked really cool—like something a teenager might have in their bedroom. But after a few months the cactus began to slump. I kept blowing it back up, but it must have had a puncture because one morning it was completely flat. Mum rolled it up and put it in a drawer and said she'd ask Gary if he thought it was worth repairing, but she never did.

On moving-in day he drove into the driveway and parked next to Mum's car. He usually parked on the street, but that day was different; on that day he was staying forever. Our home was going to be his home as well.

"Ah, that's a nice welcome party!" he called, getting out of his car as we both stood on the front doorstep, waving and grinning at him. He laughed and went to get some bags out of his trunk. Mum gave me a nudge.

"Go and give him a hand, Nate."

I walked down the drive in my slippers and held out a hand, and as a joke Gary gave me the heaviest case, which fell to the ground with a thump. We laughed, but he quickly grabbed it off me when I tried to drag it along the concrete.

"Might be an idea to get rid of your car, Fiona. We won't need two, will we? And that'll mean more space in the driveway."

Mum had had her car for years. It was a bit rusty in places, but it suited the two of us fine.

"Oh. I hadn't thought about that," said Mum. "I guess it makes sense. Let's see, shall we?"

Gary dropped his bags by the stairs and looked up and around the hallway as if he was seeing it for the first time, and then he took off his jacket and hung it over mine on a hook by the door. There was a spare hook next to Mum's coat, but perhaps he hadn't noticed it. It all went a bit quiet and then Mum gave me another nudge and I ran to the kitchen to grab the card I'd made.

"Oh wow, what's this?" he said, tearing the envelope. "You've made this? How fantastic."

I watched him as he studied the front of the card and then opened it up to read. I can't remember exactly what I wrote, but it was something about being over the moon that he was coming to live with us. On the front, I'd drawn a crescent moon with me jumping over it with splashes of glitter as the stars, which were now sprinkling down onto Gary's trousers.

"Thanks, Nate. That's really something," he said, and he put it back into the envelope and dropped it onto the stairs.

Mum put her arms around him and gave him a kiss.

"Welcome to your new home, Gary. I think we're all going to be very happy here, don't you?"

He smiled at her. "I'll just get the rest of my things."

As he walked down the drive he gave his trousers a sharp shake and the glitter fell off onto the concrete.

That night I went to bed feeling really happy. I put my light jar on like I did every evening and lay in bed and listened to them downstairs as they laughed over a comedy show on TV. I wondered if Mum might suggest they go on a quiz show together, like she'd done with Dad on *How Well Do You Know Me?* I was sure there was something they could do, perhaps one of those shows where they run around a supermarket finding things. Or maybe a show that needed you to answer lots of questions. I reckoned Gary would be good at that.

I fell asleep but woke up to the sound of Mum and Gary's voices in my room. They were in the corner, arguing in loud whispers.

"I don't care if he's your son. I can't sleep with that thing glowing all night."

"But we can't even see it in our room, Gary! Nate has never liked the dark, and it's in his room."

I peeked at them over my duvet. Mum rubbed Gary's arm, but he shook her off.

"Well, I can see it under the door, Fiona! No kids have night-lights at that age. He's eight years old, and it's about time he grew up a bit."

It went quiet for a moment, and then I heard Mum's gentle voice.

"It's not a nightlight, Gary. It's a light jar. A string of lights in a little glass jar. That's all it is."

I really didn't like the dark, so a while ago my mum had made her version of a nightlight for me—a light jar. She'd seen one on the internet and said it was the perfect answer to my fear of the dark. It also meant that if I had friends over, no one would know it was actually a nightlight because it looked too cool. She bought a small glass jar and filled it with a string of lights that had a little battery pack attached, and she placed it on the shelf. I loved my light jar. It gave the room a comforting glow, but as I liked to keep my door open, I guess it lit the hallway up a bit. That must be why Gary said he could see it from Mum's room.

"If I'm going to live here with you both, we need to compromise, don't we?" said Gary, taking the jar off the shelf. "And I need total darkness to sleep, so this has to go . . ."

He walked out of the room and everything went dark. I gasped and Mum came over to my bed.

"It's fine, Nate. Sorry we woke you up. Just roll over and go back to sleep. Okay? There's a good boy."

I heard Gary shut the bedroom door with a bang, which was odd because Mum was still inside with me.

"I don't like it, Mum. It's too dark. Can't you get it back?" I said.

Mum stroked my hair.

"Let's just leave it for now and we'll talk about it in the morning, okay? Go back to sleep."

She pecked a quick kiss on the top of my head before going to her room. Or their room. I listened hard but couldn't hear any talking and I shut my eyes tightly against the blackness. We lived on a road out of town with only two other houses and no streetlights, so when it got dark, it really, really got dark.

The next day I found the jar in pieces in the kitchen garbage.

The string of lights was in there too. Gary told Mum he'd dropped it by accident, but I knew he was lying. I asked Mum if she could make me another one and she said she would, but she never did. I don't think Gary would have liked it. I carefully took the string of lights out of the garbage, shook off the pieces of glass, and hid them under my mattress. Mum never knew I did that.

# CHAPTER 6

# THE TENNIS BALL

When I woke up, for a moment it felt like I was back in the guest room at Grandma's house. A patchwork quilt was just centimeters from my face. I stared at the colorful fabric squares. Grandma had started making a patchwork quilt once. I'd watched as she sewed ten tiny squares together, telling me how it would soon grow into a great big blanket. But then Granddad got ill and her time was taken up with going to and from the hospital.

I blinked at the quilt in front of my eyes. Maybe Grandma had finished it after all? There was a square with three strawberries on it and another with a kite, blowing in the wind. The different fabrics had been randomly sewn together. I held my breath. Grandma was using a repeating pattern: one blue, three cream, two red. This wasn't Grandma's house. I slowly pulled the quilt down and peeked over the edge. I was still in the cold, gloomy cottage. I jumped up off the sofa and ran to the window. Mum had probably come back and, not wanting to disturb me, crept upstairs to bed.

But there was no car. She hadn't returned at all.

The sky was getting light but only enough for me to know it was still very early. I went to the kitchen hoping to find a note or a bag of shopping—anything to show that she'd been here while I was asleep—but everything was exactly as it had been last night:

half a roll of mints and a few cans of food. My heart was pounding. Mum had been gone for over twelve hours. Something must have happened to her. Maybe it was Gary? Maybe he'd been following us after all? Or maybe something had happened to the car and she'd had to walk back and was just upstairs asleep. Yes—that must be what had happened. I ran up to check her room, but when I burst through the door I felt my throat tighten. Mum wasn't there. Her bed was neatly made, her bag of clothes still open on the floor where she'd left it. There was no sign that she'd been back at all. My ears began to ring and I felt dizzy, so I sat down on the sagging mattress.

"Where are you, Mum? Why aren't you here?" I said out loud.

I sat there for about half an hour, staring at a spot on the carpet and listening for any sounds of a car, but all I could hear was the wind whistling around the walls, trying to find a way in.

I looked down at her bag and put it on the bed. I needed to do something, so I decided to unpack so that Mum would be pleased when she got back. I opened the wardrobe. The musty smell wasn't good, but it looked clean enough and it was empty apart from a few hangers. I wasn't very good at hanging the clothes up, so I decided to put them in a neat pile at the bottom. I put her bag of toiletries on the chest of drawers, and then I put her little white alarm clock on the table beside the bed. There was something else at the bottom of her bag. Something wrapped in blue polka-dot paper. It was a present. I picked it up and read the tag:

*To Nate*
*All my love,*
*x Mum*

I sat down on the bed and held it in my hand. I gave it a little squeeze. The paper squished and I felt something hard underneath. Mum probably wouldn't be happy that I'd found it, so I put it back in her bag. I was just doing up the zipper when a noise from downstairs made me jump. I sat there for a moment, listening. Maybe it was a knock? Maybe it was Mum! I quickly ran down the creaky stairs, opened the living room door, and stopped.

There, in the middle of the carpet, was my tennis ball, the one I had been bouncing last night until it rolled under the sofa. I stared at the ball, trying to think how it could have gotten there. I looked at the fire, which was now cold with a layer of gray ash. Could the fire have caused a draft that had blown the tennis ball out?

I could sense something yellow glowing in the corner of the room, but I was too frightened to look. I just kept my eyes fixed on the ball. Maybe I should roll it back under the sofa and see what would happen? No. I would pick it up and put it back in my backpack.

"Hello, Nate."

I shuddered.

Someone was talking to me.

Someone wearing bright yellow was standing by the window in front of the half-closed curtains and they were talking to me.

Here.

Right now.

I was frozen to the spot.

"I got your ball back. Do you want to play catch?"

I felt dizzy. Was I dreaming? I must be dreaming. Or I was exhausted—that must be it; I was tired and hallucinating. I slowly turned my head to look.

Standing by the window with his arms folded and wearing a bright yellow T-shirt and jeans was a boy. His hair was the color of sand and his nose was covered with freckles. And he had a glow around him. A warm, yellow glow.

"Or how about hot potato! You used to love that one. Do you remember how to play?"

He took a few steps toward me and I stumbled backward.

"I—I . . . I don't understand . . ." I said, putting a hand out to the dining table to steady myself.

The boy gave me a wide smile and held his arms out as if he were about to give me a really big hug.

"It's me! I'm back!"

I blinked and blinked again as I studied his face. He'd gotten older, but it was still a face I recognized very well. Standing in the living room, in this deserted cottage, was someone who had been constantly by my side from when I was about three until I was five.

I couldn't actually remember when he left; he just sort of faded away one day.

"I can't . . . I can't . . ." I began, struggling to get my breath. "Is . . . Is that you? Is that really you?"

"Yep, it's me, all right!" he said. "Hello."

I took a big gulp of air. My ears were ringing and I felt like I was about to faint.

Standing in the corner of the room was my old imaginary friend, Sam.

# CHAPTER 7
# SAM

"I—I . . . I'm dreaming . . ." I said quietly. "Everything is fine, I'm just having a bad dream."

I sank down onto a wooden dining chair and watched him as he walked around the room. He bent over and studied all the ornaments along the mantelpiece above the wood stove, peering closely at each one and stopping at a porcelain spaniel who was gazing up at him with soppy eyes.

"Y-You're a dream, right? You're not really here at all. I'm just . . . I'm still asleep. I'm just having a dream. Aren't I?"

Sam looked at me and snorted. "Nope. I'm not a dream."

I scrunched up my eyes and opened them again, but he was still there.

"Wh-What are you doing here?" I asked.

"I told you, Nate! I'm back! Do you live here now? What happened to your old house?"

"I—I . . . We . . . We're just . . . staying for a bit . . ."

"We came here once before. Do you remember? The cowboy duvet and the maze?"

I opened my mouth and then shut it again. This really couldn't be happening.

He sat down on the sofa and picked up something that was hidden in the folds of the patchwork quilt. "Oh wow, look who it is! Mrs. Ellie-Fant! You still have her? After all this time?"

His freckled nose creased up, and he wiggled the elephant at me. I walked toward him, hesitated for a moment, and then quickly snatched the toy from him, stuffing it back into the bottom of my backpack.

"Hey! Nate!" he said, leaning forward. "Have you still got that game we used to play? The one with the little red and yellow circles where you had to get them in a row? What was it called? Connect Four!"

I held the backpack tightly against my chest. "*You* didn't play it. I was playing it. *You* weren't there. You're . . . You're imaginary, remember?"

Sam's face stayed fixed in a wide grin, but his glow seemed to fade a little. I carried on.

"I—I pretended you were there and I took your turns. Okay? You're *not* real. I made you up."

He frowned as he thought about it for a bit, and then he burst into laughter. "Oh, you're so funny, of course I was playing! How could you have played on your own? You're just saying that because I always won. You always were a bad loser."

While he chuckled to himself I ran to the hallway.

"Hey! Where are you going?"

I stuffed my feet into my sneakers and then tugged on the front door. It was stuck. Sam stood by my side, watching over my shoulder as I struggled to get out.

"What's the problem, Nate? I thought you'd be pleased to see me. It's been so long."

"Go away!"

I could feel the ice-cold air outside as my fingers gripped the edge of the door.

"How long has it been, do you think? Do you know? Do you know how long we've been apart?"

I'd managed to get the door open a bit, but there still wasn't enough room for me to get through. Sam walked around and leaned against the wall.

"This might surprise you, Nate, but did you know . . . ?" He laughed a little to himself. "Did you know that it's been six years? Six years since you decided you didn't need me anymore? How about that?"

I stopped and stared at his face. His smile was completely gone now, and he looked sad. Very sad. I gave the door a final pull and managed to squeeze out into the frozen air.

"Hey, come back! It's fine! I'm over it!"

I hurried toward the dirt track, hoping that Mum's car would be heading toward me right this second, but the road was deserted. All I could hear were the birds and the crunch of the icy ground beneath my feet. I stood and looked in the direction that Mum would be driving back from, and then I began to walk. I shivered.

My breath came in white puffs, and my ears tingled with the cold. I skidded on a frozen puddle, and the shock made me gasp out loud. I stopped for a moment to think.

None of this was making any sense. I was miles from anywhere, my mum was missing, and now my old imaginary friend was walking around and talking to me in some creepy cottage. The imaginary friend I'd made up in my head back when I was still using crayons and playing with sticker books. The one I hadn't seen for six years. This couldn't be happening.

I shivered again. I couldn't go far without my coat. What I should do was turn around and go back to the cottage. If Sam was still there, I'd just ignore him until he went away. Easy. I wouldn't look at him or speak to him and he'd give up and fade away, back to wherever he came from. My stomach gurgled like it had a plumbing problem. I still hadn't eaten anything apart from the scrambled eggs and those couple of mints yesterday. I was starving. I needed to eat, get something warmer on, and think of a plan. The door was still open when I got back, and I squeezed in through the gap and shoved it hard with my shoulder to close it once more. I could hear a tinkling sound and a voice . . .

"Oh wow, this is something else . . ."

I took my sneakers off and tucked my hands into my armpits. I was so cold. I'd have to try to get the fire going again soon or I'd freeze.

The tinkling sound got louder and more frantic as I walked back to the living room.

"No! How did you know that?!"

Sam was sitting on the sofa with my Ask Me a Question magic ball in his hand. It was going into overdrive.

"Nate! This thing is *sorcery*. I was thinking of a dog and it guessed right. Do you know that it can *actually read your mind*? This is *the* best thing I've *ever* seen."

I was about to point out that if he was thinking of something as easy as a dog, then of course the magic ball was going to guess it correctly. But then I remembered I was going to ignore him, so I shut my mouth and went through to the kitchen.

I looked through the cupboards and found more canned food, which I stacked up on one side. Potatoes, carrots, pineapple chunks. I rummaged around in the drawers until I found a can opener, and then I set to work trying to open the creamed rice. I knew you could eat that cold. I usually liked it warm with a blob of strawberry jam swirled in the middle, but there wasn't any jam and I didn't fancy using the stove, so I'd just have to eat it as it was. The opener slipped and I couldn't get it to stay on the can.

"You've got to turn the wheel to get it to grip."

I jumped. Sam was behind me, watching.

"Once you've punctured a hole it'll be easier. Just keep turning."

I did what he said but didn't look at him. The can kept skidding on the kitchen counter. Sam pointed at a tea towel on the work surface in front of me.

"Stand it on that to stop it from slipping."

I took a couple of deep breaths as I angled the opener on the side of the can again. The tea towel helped to keep the can steady, and I slowly turned the wheel until I'd made a jagged circle. It was open.

I got a bowl from the cupboard and rinsed it under the tap.

"I think you should leave half for later, don't you? Don't eat it all in one go. You'll have something for lunch then."

I spooned some of the rice into the bowl.

"That's it. Perfect. Oh, why are you crying?"

I put the spoon down and wiped my eyes. "I'm not. Go away."

"There's no need to cry. *I'm* here now," he said. I looked at him. There was something about seeing his face again that made me feel safer, just for a moment.

I walked around him and took the bowl into the front room, then sat on the sofa beside the stone-cold fire and began to eat.

"I don't know why you're so upset about me being here. We used to be friends. Best friends! Do you remember all those fun times we had?"

I carried on ignoring him and ate my rice. It was sickly sweet, but I was too hungry to care. Sam sighed, then picked up the Ask Me a Question magic ball again and pressed START.

"Could you stop playing with my things?" I said, glaring at him.

He looked at me and then turned it off and put it down. I wiped my eyes.

"I don't understand. You're not real; you're imaginary. You're in my head, but I can't make you go away. Why won't you go away?"

Sam leaned toward me. The yellow of his T-shirt made a warm, buttercup glow under his chin.

"I'm here because you want me to be, Nate. Isn't that fantastic?"

He had grown up over the past six years, just like I had, but he looked so alive, so well, and so unbelievably happy. He looked the opposite of how I was feeling. I couldn't understand why he'd come back or why I couldn't make him go away, but if he wasn't here, then I'd be all on my own again. On my own in a freezing cold, dark cottage.

I squeezed my eyes together to get the last tear away and took a deep breath.

"You're wrong, you know. About what you said earlier."

Sam frowned at me, resting his head on his hand. "Wrong about what, exactly?"

I licked the last of the creamed rice off the spoon and let it clatter into the bowl. "That game you said I was a poor loser at? Connect Four?"

He nodded. "Yes. What about it?"

"It was me who won. *Every* time."

Sam looked at me and grinned.

# CHAPTER 8
# A STRANGER IN THE WOOD

According to my book *Freaky Things to Freak You Out*, there are five keys to success if you find yourself in a survival-against-the-odds situation:

1) Shelter
2) Water
3) Food
4) Fire
5) Attitude

*In 1978, Jonah White survived three weeks in a Canadian forest by drinking from a stream and eating lichen. At night he climbed a tree and slept along a branch, hoping to avoid any passing bears looking for a midnight feast! He was discovered by Mary Judge, who ran the visitor center café just eight hundred yards away. Ms. Judge commented: "Why, if Mr. White had just taken a moment to survey his immediate vicinity, he could have realized that we were just around the corner." A red-faced Jonah White remarked: "I thought I could smell coffee and pancakes every morning, but figured I must have been dreaming . . ."*

*How about that, readers, for Survival of the Dumbest?*

There was a picture of Jonah White looking grubby and very embarrassed as he sat at a picnic table eating pancakes.

Mary Judge was standing next to him with her hand on his shoulder. Her eyebrows were raised as if to say, *Can you believe this idiot?*

I looked at the survival list again. I was fine for shelter and water, and I was pretty sure I could get the fire lit. As for food, I had a few cans to keep me going, so that just left attitude. I had to be positive.

I was sure Mum would be back before long, but in the meantime, it wouldn't hurt to do what Jonah had failed to do: survey my immediate vicinity.

Sam watched me as I got ready to go outside.

"I thought the whole point was to stay hidden. To stay inside," he said.

I zipped up my coat and pulled the sleeves down as far as I could.

"I won't be long. I'm just going to take a look out back and see what's around."

Sam sat on the sofa and flipped through my book. I wasn't sure how to deal with him at the moment, so for now I just planned to go along with things.

Sam got to the page with the "Say colorful/I love you" bit and he got up and looked at himself in the mirror, mouthing the words to himself.

*Colorful.*

*I love you.*

*Colorful.*

*I love you.*

His face was beaming.

"Cool! This is the best book ever!"

I smiled as he sat back down and carried on reading.

---

Outside, the air was so cold it hurt when I breathed in. The garden where Mum and I had laughed as we hit the heavy rug was now dusted with white frost, and I crunched my way through the weeds and overgrown plants to the iron gate set in the wall. The handle was stiff, but the gate swung open with a loud creak and then clattered shut behind me. A few crows cawed and swept up into the trees as I walked into the woods. It was slightly warmer under here out of the wind, and the ground was springy and not frozen like the garden. I looked around. Hanging motionless from one of the branches of a tree was an old black tire. I walked toward it and gave it a little push, and the long rope creaked against the branch.

"You do realize that you are trespassing, don't you?"

I froze. There was someone in the woods with me. For a moment I considered running back to the cottage, but that might have looked suspicious, so I stood my ground. A girl appeared from behind a tree and walked toward me. She had long brown hair and was wearing a navy-blue woolly hat that had been pulled down so low she had to tip her head back to see where she was going. Over one shoulder she had a canvas satchel, and she was dragging a large shovel along beside her.

"What are you doing here?" she asked.

"Sorry. I—I'm staying in the cottage. I'm on . . . I'm on holiday."

I pointed in the direction of the garden, as if she didn't know where it was.

"A holiday? In that place?"

The end of her nose was pale blue. She looked absolutely freezing.

"We're just staying there for a few days to, erm, help clean the place up."

She stood the shovel in front of her and leaned on the handle.

"That doesn't sound like much of a holiday to me."

I wondered if running now would be a wise thing to do. I'd promised Mum I wouldn't give us away, and I'd managed to fail pretty immediately.

"It's a working holiday. My parents are, erm, interior designers. They're renovating the cottage."

I'd managed three lies in one sentence and given her the red herring that there were three of us, so I felt a bit better.

"Well, the woods are private land, so you shouldn't really be in here."

She folded her arms and scowled, but the shovel fell on the ground and kind of spoiled her moment.

"Fair enough," I said. I turned to go back.

"Wait a minute! Aren't you going to ask me what I'm doing?"

I stopped. "I'm sorry?"

The girl quickly picked up the shovel.

"With this, I mean!" she said, waving the shovel at me. "Surely you're curious? Aren't you wondering what I'm doing in the woods, digging? What if I'm burying a dead body or something?"

Her eyes narrowed, her lips pursed together tightly. The cold air was pinching at my ears, and I just wanted to get back inside and get the fire going.

"If you were burying a body, I don't think you would have called out to me, unless you were really, really stupid. Plus, there are far too many roots around here for you to get deep enough, even if the ground wasn't frozen solid. You'll need to go down at least a meter or two to hide a body, and to be honest, with that shovel and without the right tools, you've got no hope."

Her mouth dangled open. I thought I'd said enough, so I turned back to the gate.

"Hold on! I didn't mean it. I'm not digging a grave, *obviously*. I'm looking for something. Something really, really precious."

I pushed the gate open, hoping she wouldn't follow.

"Well, aren't you going to ask me what it is?" she said, catching up with me. "Don't you want to know what I'm looking for?"

"No, not really," I said.

The woolly hat had slipped even farther down, and she pushed it out of her eyes. Her lips looked almost blue. She scowled.

"It's treasure, if you must know," she said.

She sniffed and tried to twirl the shovel casually, but it was far too big and too heavy and she dropped it again with a clang. This time she left it there and took a few steps toward me.

"I'm Kitty," she said, holding out a muddy hand.

I'd never shaken hands with anyone my age before, and I wasn't going to start now. I folded my arms and just nodded at her.

"Nate," I said, then instantly regretted not using a false name. "Well, I'd better be going," I continued hurriedly. "My mum and dad are cooking a big meal and . . . I need to . . . set the table. Good luck with finding the treasure."

She twisted her head to look over my shoulder at the cottage and started to say something else, but I quickly scurried through the gate, closing it with a loud squeak. I went in through the back door into the kitchen. There was no sign of Sam.

I checked the front of the house again, just in case Mum had returned and I hadn't heard the car, but the driveway was empty. I kept my coat on and tried lighting the fire. I raked the ash so that it was flat and broke off two matches from a packet near the basket of wood. I then layered some small pieces of wood on top, pushed the little vents on the stove to the left, and lit a match. The flames caught instantly and singed the top of my thumb. I quickly shut the door with the handle I'd seen Mum use, then went to the kitchen and ran the tap, putting my stinging thumb in the cold water. It throbbed for a bit before going numb. I looked up and jumped. There was a face, staring at me from the kitchen window.

"Hello again! I was wondering if you fancy helping me? Considering how you know about digging and all that?"

It was the girl from the woods. She'd followed me.

I shook my head at her, but she just blinked at me as if she hadn't noticed.

I turned the tap off and opened the back door with a huff.

"Oh, have your parents not started dinner yet?" she said, peering in.

"No. They've just gone out to get some more . . . some more potatoes. We've run out."

She nodded and we both stood in silence for a moment, but I could feel the lie making my face go red.

"The head gardener to the house, William, used to live here. The gate you came through is known as William's Gate, and that's how he used to come to work each day. He was given the cottage when he retired, and he never really went out after that. He died on the sofa, apparently."

Great. As if things in here weren't bad enough, I now had to think about dead bodies on the sofa. She looked so pleased with herself for knowing all this stuff that I couldn't resist chipping in.

"William was my grandma's friend, actually. They went to school together."

Kitty shifted from one foot to another and chewed on her lip. She didn't look happy that I was in the know about something around here.

"Ah, I see. But I don't expect you know that William used to create treasure hunts when he was younger, did you?"

I shrugged. Mum had mentioned it before, but I didn't know much about them. I let Kitty carry on.

"He used to make them up for James and Charlotte. They loved them. He stopped doing them though. After the accident."

"Who were James and Charlotte?" I asked. "And what accident?"

She looked at me for a long moment before answering.

"James is my dad and Charlotte's his sister. William made little individual treasure hunts for each of them with three clues, leaving a special gift at the end. They'd always solve them together. But there was one they never completed. One for Charlotte."

She trailed off and pursed her lips together as if she'd said too much. It was odd she called her dad by his first name, but she was quite posh and I think posh people do that sometimes.

"It can get kind of lonely living here, you know? I think he liked to make up these little puzzles to keep himself busy. It gave him something to do when he wasn't working. He didn't really have anyone else nearby besides my family. But I guess you know that already if he was a friend of your grandma's."

I nodded as if I was interested, but really I was trying to think of a way to get rid of her.

"I'm trying to solve the last treasure hunt he ever made. It was never solved, you see. I've been searching for the next clue for weeks, but I can't find it."

"Weeks, eh?" I said. "Couldn't you have just asked William what the clues meant? Before he died?"

Kitty looked at me as if I'd said the most ridiculous thing ever.

"No! Like I said before, he was a private man, and after he retired he just hid himself away in this cottage. He *never* welcomed visitors. And anyway, if I'd asked him for the answers, then that would have been cheating, wouldn't it?"

I held on to the edge of the door, getting ready to close it. I'd had enough of her.

"Anyway, good luck with it," I said, but she ignored the hint.

"I just want to show you the first clue. I'll only take a minute. It might make more sense to you, seeing that you know so much stuff. I mean, look what you've taught me already about burying dead bodies!"

I shrugged.

"Well, I don't know . . ."

Kitty reached into her coat pocket and took out a piece of paper. It looked old. "This is the first clue, and I've just got no idea where to look next."

She held it up and I read the handwritten scrawl out loud.

CLUE 1

I'M A THOUSAND YEARS OLD, YET STILL STRONG AS LEAD

I'M SYMBOLIC OF LIFE, YET WATCH OVER THE DEAD.

MY ROOTS THEY ARE DEEP, THEY ARE SOLID AND TRUE,

IF YOU SEEK ME OUT NOW, YOU WILL FIND THE NEXT CLUE.

I felt the hairs stand up on the back of my neck.

"It sounds like some kind of tree to me," I said.

"I know that," she said, rolling her eyes. "But do you have any idea how many trees there are out there? Hundreds!"

Suddenly her face lit up.

"Maybe we could search for the treasure together. Wouldn't that be great? Just like my dad and Charlotte used to! We could start by looking around the cottage. See if old William left any extra clues lying around."

She stretched up to peek over my shoulder into the kitchen.

"He might have written the solution down somewhere. Maybe on a scrap of paper or tucked into a book or something? Actually, that's a really good idea, if I don't say so myself! We should check *all* of the books! We should go through each one and give them a good shake for any hidden clues."

I had no intention of doing anything of the sort, but she wasn't taking my huge hints that I wanted to be left alone.

"So, how about it? I'm sure your parents won't mind. That was William's bedroom up there."

She pointed at the room above the kitchen where my mum had slept for just one night.

I couldn't let her in. She might work out that I was on my own.

"Hold on," I said. "The woods belong to your family, but the cottage belongs to William's family now?"

She nodded.

I folded my arms. "So technically you're trespassing by being here then. Aren't you?"

Her bottom lip jutted out. "Well, no. Not really. I was just seeing if you wanted to help with the riddle and the treasure."

I pretended to consider it, looking up to one side and tapping my chin with my finger. "Erm, no. But what I do want you to do is get off this property."

I gave her my best glare.

"But . . . But it won't take five minutes. And it's to help me."

"But I don't even know you. And anyway, surely you have servants to do this kind of work for you? Can't Daddy hire a private investigator or something?"

She looked astounded that I was talking to her in this way, and to be honest with you, so was I. I'd never been quite this rude to someone before, but I needed to get rid of her. I'd promised Mum that I'd lie low. She pulled her hat tightly over her ears and picked up the shovel.

"Fine. Forget it. Forget I ever asked. Enjoy your *holiday*, Nate."

She took a couple of steps backward, glaring at me, and then turned away, dragging the shovel along the concrete path as she went.

"You handled that well," said Sam, walking in from the living room. I frowned at him.

"What are you doing here? I can't believe I was so stupid talking to her in the first place. If . . . If it gets back to anyone that we are here . . . What was I thinking?"

I paced up and down the kitchen as Sam watched me.

"I even told her my name! I'm an idiot, Sam. An absolute idiot!"

Sam was glowing so brightly that he was making my eyes water. "I don't think you've got anything to worry about there. She's just a bit of a lost soul. It must be lonely living in that big house with no one for miles around."

I felt a bit guilty then. Perhaps I should have told Kitty about Mum being missing; she could have gotten her dad, James, to help find her. But I'd told Mum that I wouldn't give away that we were here. If Gary found out where we were, then . . . then it'd be bad. Really, really bad.

"What are you going to do about your mum?" asked Sam, as if he could read my thoughts. "She might need your help. Something might have happened to her, Nate."

I didn't want to hear that.

"No, it hasn't. I've just got to give her more time, that's all. She'll be back; I know it. She's probably just sorting out a few things. Maybe she's looking for somewhere better than this dump. She knows how much I don't want to stay here."

Sam watched as I paced up and down.

"I can't break my promise, Sam. Not after everything she's been through."

I went back into the living room and carefully put another log on the fire. The burn on my thumb was throbbing again. Sam stood behind me.

"You can't just hope that she's going to turn up, you know."

"Look, go away, would you? No one asked you to come back. In fact, what are you even doing here?"

Sam's bright yellow glow faded, and he looked a bit tearful.

"But it was you that wanted me here, Nate. That's why I came back. *You* wanted me. I wouldn't be here if you didn't. I *couldn't* be here."

I rubbed at my face. None of this was making any sense. Mum's disappearance, Sam coming back, meeting Kitty the crazy treasure hunter. It was all too much. I lay down on the patchwork quilt on the sofa and curled up, watching the flames slowly spread along the log.

"This is all Grandma's fault. All of it," I said quietly. "Me and Mum being here in the first place, it's *her* fault."

Sam came over and sat on the floor beside me, leaning against the sofa as he hugged his knees.

"Why?" he asked. "Why is all of this your grandma's fault?"

I looked at Sam, the fire reflected in his eyes, and I told him.

# CHAPTER 9
# GRANDMA

We had left Gary once before, over a year ago now.

I hadn't realized it, but Mum had been planning it for a while. She'd packed some bags while I was at school and hidden them in the trunk of her car. This was back when she still had a car, before Gary sold it.

I remember that Mum kept staring at the clock on the living room wall. Gary went to play squash every Thursday evening, but on this particular Thursday he didn't seem to be in any rush to go. I was trying to catch her eye to get her to stop looking at the time, as I was worried Gary would notice, and sometimes when he notices things he doesn't like, the air goes all prickly. It's like there is an electrical current fizzing around us. On this Thursday, Gary was still sitting in the armchair watching TV at six thirty, which was usually when he got ready.

"Are you going to play squash tonight, Gary?" I asked.

He looked up and blinked a few times, as if he was trying to remember where I'd come from.

"I—I thought you played squash on Thursdays?" I said.

Gary frowned and I instantly regretted what I'd said. I had never shown an interest in squash before. Why was I starting now?

But I was just trying to jog his memory that he was supposed to be getting changed.

He continued to stare at me, and then he got out of the armchair and headed upstairs. I could hear him moving around in the bedroom, opening drawers and then the wardrobe, and then he came back down wearing his white shorts and T-shirt.

He put his racket bag over his shoulder, stared at me again, and left without a word. It was clearly one of his silent days, when he didn't actually speak to either of us. But that was just fine, because now he was out of the house and Mum relaxed a little.

We got to Grandma's at eight o'clock. Granddad was poorly and I knew that Grandma had phoned a number of times, asking for Mum's help. I'd heard Mum say she wasn't able to get there that day or that she was too busy, but it sounded to me like she was making excuses. She wasn't very busy as far as I could tell. In fact, she rarely left the house at all any more.

When Grandma answered the door, Mum went to give her a hug, but Grandma just folded her arms.

"Oh, so now you show up. Is it too much to ask for my own daughter's help?"

Mum's mouth hung open, but Grandma just turned and went inside. I didn't like it. I had never seen Grandma angry before. We both had a suitcase each, and we struggled over the high step and put them side by side in the hall. A strong smell of disinfectant made my eyes water, and I could hear a quiet humming coming from upstairs.

"I'm sorry, Mum. Okay? I'm here now. I just couldn't get away . . . You know how Gary can be . . . How's Dad?" said Mum, following Grandma toward the kitchen.

Grandma fell into a kitchen chair. Her arms dangled down by her sides as if she didn't even have enough energy to hold them folded in her lap. Her gray sweater with the sequined heart on the front had stains down it, and her hair was all over the place. She looked like she hadn't slept properly in weeks.

"I've been doing this practically single-handed, Fiona. Do you know how hard it is? Being a caretaker? Have you any idea? I've needed you and I've needed your help. Where have you been?"

"I'm sorry, Mum. But . . . things haven't been easy . . . at home . . ."

This seemed to make Grandma even more angry.

"Oh, I'm so sorry *you've* had a rough time, Fiona. Have you any idea how it's been for me? Nursing your father all these weeks? And now you turn up expecting to be welcomed with open arms? Well, I'm not doing it!"

I'd never seen Grandma like this. Her eyes were wide and she looked a bit scary. Mum was sitting hunched over the kitchen table. She seemed to be folding up into herself. I waited for her to say something, but she just hung her head and shook it slightly.

"I'm sorry. I'm so sorry I've not been here, but it's . . . Things have been difficult . . . at home . . . with . . . with Gary. He's not . . . He's not the man I thought he was. It's not the life I imagined, Mum."

She looked up. Her face was all crumpled and I knew she was close to tears, but Grandma didn't seem to care.

"Not the life you imagined?" she said, and she even gave a little chuckle, but it was brittle and there was no warmth behind it. *"Not the life you imagined?* Don't make me laugh . . . Everyone has relationship problems, Fiona. It doesn't mean you forget your blood and bones. Do you think I imagined I'd be living like this? Nursing your father?"

She stood up abruptly, the chair scraping noisily behind her, but her face softened when she saw me by the door. I think she'd forgotten I was there.

"Nate, be a good boy and pop upstairs and say hello to Granddad, would you? He'd love to see you. Your mum and I are going to have a little chat."

She turned to fill the kettle, and I put a hand on Mum's shoulder. She turned and looked up at me, her face pinched and worried. I frowned. *What is going on?*

Mum patted my hand and mouthed, *It's okay.*

Going up to see Granddad was possibly the last thing in the whole wide world that I wanted to do. I did think about just staying in the hallway and listening to what was being said in the kitchen, but if Grandma had found me, in the mood she was in, she'd have gone mad. Mum got up and closed the kitchen door behind me as the kettle rumbled away.

The stairs to Grandma and Granddad's bedroom were heavily carpeted, and my walk to the top was soundless. The humming noise I'd heard when we'd first arrived was getting louder, and when I looked through the crack in the bedroom door I saw the corner of a hospital bed that had been squeezed in beside their wardrobe. A pink bedspread was folded across Granddad's feet as if Grandma had been trying to make it look like part of the furniture. It had been raised at one end, and Granddad was lying back on some pillows, his chest slowly rising, up and down. His index finger picked at the edge of his thumb, so I knew he was awake. I stepped into the room, and he opened his eyes.

"Nathaniel! How lovely to see you. Come over here and take a seat."

He patted at the mattress, and I perched on the edge as far away from him as I could. I wasn't being rude; I just didn't want to get any closer.

"How have you been? All okay at school? How's the cricket coming along?"

Granddad loved cricket. A few summers ago, before he became ill, he'd taught me how to bowl in their back garden.

"It's going well, Granddad. It's all good."

I actually hadn't touched a cricket ball since, but I didn't want to disappoint him.

He closed his eyes and patted his hand on the bed. I wasn't sure if he wanted me to move closer, but I stayed where I was.

"And how's that spin bowl of yours coming along?" A wide smile spread across his face. "Do you remember that cracker you

66

did? I tried to get my bat on it, but *whoosh* . . . it just flew off, into the bushes. Couldn't get anywhere near it!"

He laughed and I wondered if he was replaying everything on the back of his eyelids, like a little movie.

"Never did find that ball, you know. Never found it!" He laughed again. "We gave up after that and went inside, and Grandma made you your first knickerbocker glory. Do you remember? Your eyes were as big as saucers!"

I remembered that bit very well. It was in a tall, frosted glass with swirls and swirls of strawberry sauce and a fan-shaped wafer poking out of the top. I had to kneel on the kitchen chair and use a special long spoon to eat it. After that, she started making them for me every time we visited. That weekend playing cricket with Granddad was beginning to come back to me a bit more now. Mum and Dad were still together back then, and they'd gone to a wedding and I'd stayed with Grandma and Granddad right up until Sunday evening. They'd let me stay up late and watch a movie with them, *and* I ate two bowls of popcorn even though I'd already brushed my teeth for bed. I was about to ask Granddad if he could remember the movie we'd watched when Mum appeared in the doorway.

"Nate? Can you go downstairs while I just say hello to Granddad? We'll be going home in a minute."

I couldn't believe it. *Home?* We'd only just arrived. I wanted to stay here, with Grandma and Granddad, where the air didn't prickle. Mum's eyes were red and she wouldn't look directly at me.

"But," I said as I joined her in the doorway. "But I thought we were staying? We've got our bags and things."

Mum looked toward Granddad and shook her head sharply, then pushed past me into the bedroom.

"Hello, Dad," she said, and she sat beside him. He reached up and stroked her hair.

"Hello, darling," he said.

I went silently back downstairs. I could hear Grandma moving about in the kitchen, but I didn't want to see her. The heavy suitcases that we'd dragged into the hallway had been moved. Now they were right beside the door.

---

Sam hadn't said a word while I told him about Grandma not letting us stay. He was still sitting on the floor, hugging his knees.

"That must have hurt big-time," he said.

I shrugged. I didn't want to cry, so I didn't say anything.

"It *really* hurts, doesn't it? Not being wanted. Not being able to stay. Feeling like you have nowhere to go."

He was looking at me sadly. I wasn't sure what he was getting at, but it felt like it had something to do with when he faded away when I was younger.

His face suddenly brightened and his glow returned.

"But hey. Here we are! You're here, and I'm here, and all is good. The others are going to be so jealous when I tell them."

"Others?" I asked, sitting back upright. "What do you mean, the others? Do you mean there are more? There are more like you?"

Sam nodded. "Yes. Their friends grew up too. Just like you did. And when that happens . . . When we're not needed any longer, we just kind of . . . drift until we're needed. It's so *boring*."

"Drift? What do you mean, drift? What, like . . . like ghosts?"

I looked around the room, terrified that at any moment something was going to appear.

Sam frowned. "No, not ghosts exactly . . ."

"Wh-What do you mean, not exactly? What are you, Sam?"

I knew I was shouting, but I couldn't help it. My legs began to shake, so I held onto my knees.

Sam seemed to think about it for a moment, and then his face broke into his wide grin.

"We're like . . . helpers. We turn up when you're little. When you have open minds and don't judge everything you can see. We keep you company for a bit and set you off on your way . . . and then you just get on with the rest of your lives. That's usually how it works. We don't really come back, unless . . . Well, unless you've gotten yourself into a bit of a mess."

I tried to process what he was saying.

"So . . . you're like . . . guardian angels?"

Sam frowned as he thought about it, and then his yellow glow became stronger and stronger, until it was illuminating the whole room.

"Whoa . . . What's happening? What's happening to you?!" I said as I pressed myself back into the chair.

"I'll show you," said Sam, his color brightening so much I had to shield my eyes with my hand. He waved at the wall and everything began to dissolve.

# CHAPTER 10

# AMY AND MEENA

My eyes stretched wide as the wall of the cottage evaporated and was replaced with what looked like a shimmering screen, a wavy space where the wall once was, with images beginning to form on it. I felt my jaw dangle open as I stared.

"You're not gonna faint or anything, are you?" asked Sam, still glowing.

I shook my head as I gawked at the image that was developing right in front of my eyes. The colors and shapes were merging together, finding their correct places, until the picture became something I could understand.

It was a room. A bedroom. There was a young girl laying down with her head on her arm. It looked like she was crying. Behind her was another girl, but this one wasn't like the girl on the bed. This girl had a glow about her, like Sam, but her color was purple.

"C-Can they see us?" I whispered.

Sam sat down next to me. "Nope. Can't see a thing."

A red-and-white-striped box of popcorn had appeared in his hand as if he was watching a movie. He pointed it toward me. I shook my head.

"The girl on the bed is Amy, and that's Meena behind her.

She's one of the best make-believes we have. The way she handled this situation is just . . . Well, see for yourself . . ."

He stuffed a handful of popcorn in his mouth and munched loudly. The girl on the bed, Amy, lifted her head slightly.

"They . . . They just don't understand. I hate it. And I hate them."

I turned to Sam. "What is it? Who does she hate?"

But Sam just put his fingers to his lips and nodded toward the image. "Shhhh. Just watch."

The imaginary friend glowed brightly as she sat down beside Amy on the bed.

"You need to tell them why you didn't turn up to the play, Amy. Then they'll understand. You can't expect them to understand if they don't know the full picture."

Amy rubbed her nose, her shoulders shaking.

"They said I was a loser. They said . . . They said I had let them down and they'd never forgive me . . ."

She broke down into loud sobs and put her head back on her arm.

Sam leaned toward me. "Amy had the lead part in the school play, but she didn't arrive for the evening performance."

He brushed some popcorn off his yellow T-shirt.

"Her friends are really angry with her. The whole thing had to be canceled, as they didn't have an understudy. The headmaster made an announcement and had to send the audience home."

I folded my arms as I watched Amy crying. "Well, I can understand why they were so angry. She spoiled it for everybody! I don't blame her friends for calling her a loser."

I could feel Sam staring at me, and I glanced toward him.

"So, if I was to tell you that Amy's mum had lost yet another job that day, would you think differently?"

I shrugged. The popcorn container had vanished from his hand. He looked all serious.

"And if I was to tell you that her mum was really upset, and I mean *really* upset, and she was crying about how they were going to pay the rent and buy food, would that change your mind?"

I opened my mouth to say something but shut it again.

"And what if you knew that Amy had a baby brother who was just a year old? And because her mum was so upset she'd locked herself in her bedroom, and it was up to Amy to give her little brother his dinner and give him a bath and put him to bed. Would you think she had let her friends down then?"

I looked back at the bedroom and at the girl crying on the bed. I wanted to talk to her, to tell her it was all going to be okay, but I couldn't.

"Amy's mum struggles, Nate. She doesn't always manage to do things that other parents do, so Amy makes up for it. She cleans the house, she cooks dinner, she does the dishes. And you know what? She's eight."

Amy was sitting up now. She'd stopped crying, and Meena, the imaginary friend, was sitting beside her, talking in whispers.

"What's Meena doing?"

Sam smiled. "Her job," he said proudly.

The little girl listened and wiped her nose on her sleeve as her imaginary friend whispered into her ear. Her shoulders were still trembling from her crying, but she was definitely calming down.

"Okay, okay, so Amy's having a tough time. I get it. So why didn't she tell her friends and teachers that this was why she couldn't be in the play? Why doesn't she tell someone what's going on?"

I turned to face Sam. He seemed to have aged slightly, and his eyes were a deep amber.

"Not everyone wants to tell other people their business, do they, Nate? Just like your mum didn't want to tell your grandma about Gary. Remember? Sometimes people might appear to walk tall, but on their shoulders they could be carrying an incredibly heavy load that you know nothing about."

I blinked back at him. He was right. It wasn't Grandma's fault that she hadn't let us stay that day. She didn't know how bad things were with Gary—how could she if Mum hadn't said anything?

I looked back at the wall but was faced with the scruffy, peeling paint and cobwebs that had been there a few moments ago. Amy and Meena were gone. I turned to ask Sam what had happened to Amy, but he'd disappeared too.

# CHAPTER 11
# HELPING KITTY

I found a packet of rice in the back of a kitchen cupboard, and I held on to it as I stared out of the kitchen window. Sam had been gone for nearly an hour now, so I was all on my own again. I'd been thinking about Amy and how sad she'd looked. If only she'd told her friends what was going on, then maybe they would have understood. Then they wouldn't have been so angry with her. I don't think Grandma would have been so angry with Mum if she'd known why we'd turned up with our bags on that day. I wished I could tell her. I wished I could talk to Mum. It was nearly twenty-four hours since she'd gone out for food. Maybe I should go and find the big house and tell Kitty what happened. But then she'd tell her parents and then they'd want to call the police and then I might get sent back to Gary.

I couldn't risk it. I had to give Mum more time. She was probably just making plans. Trying to find somewhere better for us to live. But she wouldn't have done that without telling me, surely? My eyes prickled with tears. Nothing was making sense. Mum always did her best for me, so maybe she was planning a nice surprise. A new home and a new town where I could have some friends over. I hadn't had anyone over since Gary moved in. Well, I did once. Kyle Gibson . . .

_____

Kyle's mum had asked my mum if he could come to us for tea, as she had a meeting after work. He was the funniest boy in my year and I'd been trying to be his friend for months, so I was really pleased. At break time we started talking about what we would do and we decided to watch *Back to the Future* on DVD (which he'd never seen), and then we'd go to my room and listen to music on his phone.

We walked home from school, kicking a stone between us all the way, which was farther than I'd ever managed on my own. When the stone reached my driveway we both cheered and danced around, but then I stopped when I saw Gary's car. He'd been living with us for a few months then.

"What's he doing here?" I said. The front door opened and Gary appeared, beaming.

"Hi, guys! How you doing? You both have a good day at school?"

We went inside and kicked off our shoes, and Kyle threw his coat on the stairs. I quickly grabbed it and hung it up with mine. Gary hated it when things were left lying around.

"Aren't you supposed to be at work?" I said.

Gary stared at me, wearing a fixed grin.

"I left early."

He turned away.

"So, you must be Kyle," he said, holding out his hand. "I'm Gary. Pleased to meet you."

Kyle gazed at the hand and then at me, and he rolled his eyes as they shook.

"Where's Mum?" I said, looking down the hall toward the kitchen.

"I've sent her out for snacks. Popcorn, tortilla chips, and lemonade!" he said, rubbing his hands together. "You can't have a friend over without snacks, can you, Nate?"

I stared at him as he slapped me on my back. I'd never seen him like this before. He was being . . . weird. And the whole "shaking Kyle's hand" thing was just embarrassing.

"I've got the Monopoly set ready on the dining table, and then I thought we'd have a game in the garden. Do you like soccer, Kyle?"

Kyle's jaw was hanging down.

"Errr . . . Yeah. Guess so."

I felt light-headed. This wasn't what I'd planned at all. Gary wasn't leaving us alone.

"It's okay; we're going to watch a movie. Come on, Kyle," I said, going into the living room.

I'd left the DVD by the TV that morning, but it was gone.

"Where's *Back to the Future*?" I asked. "I put it right here."

Gary stuck out his bottom lip and shrugged. Kyle looked at me and then at Gary.

"Monopoly it is then!" said Gary, clapping his hands together. "I thought I could be the top hat. Kyle, you can be the racing car, and Nate, you can be the thimble."

He went over to the table, and the three pieces had been lined up already. Kyle stared at me. I didn't know what to do. The air had gone all prickly again.

"Well . . . Maybe one game?" I said. "Is that okay?" I forced a smile at Kyle, who just looked horrified.

We played the game in near silence, and then Mum burst in about an hour later with a plastic bag full of snacks.

"Ah, here she is! I thought you'd gotten lost or something, Fiona. There're two boys here dying for some popcorn. Aren't you, boys?"

Kyle kept looking at me, his eyebrows nearly disappearing into his hair. All I could do was smile weakly.

"Sorry," said Mum, nervously. "The register I was at broke down and I had to go to another aisle and . . ."

"Oh, I don't think we need to know all the boring details, do we?" said Gary, laughing. Kyle snorted and then he stifled a yawn. My stomach ached from all the clenching.

The game went on for nearly three hours. I tried my hardest to lose, so that at least Kyle and I could go and listen to some music, but Gary wasn't having any of it. As he was the banker he kept giving me loans and making up stupid rules, like if you got a six you were given two hundred pounds. Mum tried to help and suggested we stop for pizza, but Gary said we could eat while we played, although he glared at me when I dropped a piece of pep-peroni on the "jail" square.

Kyle spent most of the game staring out the front window, and as soon as his mum pulled up he shot out to the hall and stuffed his shoes on.

"See ya, Nate," he said, opening the door and running down the driveway.

Gary got up and slammed the door behind him.

"Such a rude boy. Not even a thank-you," he said. I ran up to my room.

I talked to Mum that night, telling her how Gary had spoiled the whole evening, but she just dismissed me. "He was only trying to make it nice for you, Nate. You know how he is." The next day at school everyone was whispering behind their hands and pretending they weren't. In French I overheard Kyle talking to Declan, and I caught the words *Gary*, *Monopoly*, and *psycho* before they turned around and giggled at me. I didn't ask anyone else over after that.

———————————

I looked back down at the instructions on the rice. It looked like you had to weigh some out first and then measure the water. I couldn't find any measuring cups, so I'd just have to guess. I was starving. I found a small pan and ran the cold tap and waited for the murky water to clear, and then I put it on the stove and turned the knob. It lit after the third click, and the purple flames roared as if they were thrilled with being released at last.

I stared out at the garden and the forest beyond and wondered if Kitty was still out there, randomly digging her holes. The trees sparkled with the frost that covered their bare branches. Nothing moved. The whole garden was frozen, like a black-and-white photograph.

Suddenly I realized that I knew the answer to Kitty's riddle. It was there, on one line, staring her right in the face: *I'm symbolic of life, yet watch over the dead.*

Well, I wasn't going to go out of my way to tell her I'd worked it out.

Tiny bubbles began to form on the water in the saucepan. I got ready to tip the rice in but stopped when I saw something moving outside. Next to the old iron gate was a large bush, and it appeared to be shaking. There must be something hiding underneath it. I turned the burner off and leaned toward the window. What was it? Could someone fit under there? Was there enough space for someone to hide? Someone like Gary, maybe? I was just going to check if the kitchen door was locked when the bush gave a final shudder and out popped the chicken. My shoulders dropped and I breathed a big sigh of relief. I watched as the chicken scratched around on the frosty earth, her beak stabbing at the frozen soil. I thought about the survival skills in my book. If I caught the chicken, then I'd have eggs. I mean, *we'd* have eggs. It would be a nice surprise for when Mum got back. And I knew how to boil eggs.

I grabbed my coat and sneakers, but when I stepped into the garden the chicken squeezed herself through the iron gate and into

Kitty's woods. I crunched along as quietly as I could, but the gate gave a strangled squeak as I opened it and the chicken fluttered farther away. She scratched at the leaves on the woodland floor and her head stabbed at the occasional grub, but she kept one yellow eye watching me. I walked slowly, my arms outstretched.

I dove for the chicken again and again, but even though she looked incredibly slow and stupid, she always managed to be just out of reach. Then I spotted Kitty, sitting on a log wearing her thick woolly hat. Her satchel was hanging from a branch and her shovel was lying on the ground and she was studying her piece of paper.

She hadn't seen me and I wanted to keep it that way.

I dove for the chicken one last time, but this time she let out a squawk and scurried underneath some ferns.

Kitty's head darted around.

"Nate! You've come to help! That's fantastic."

I shook my head, but before I had a chance to say I had no intention of helping, she waved the clue at me.

"I still don't understand. It must be hidden beneath a tree, but I'm not getting anywhere. Look."

Next to her was a shallow hole with a web of tree roots at the bottom. I'd been right: It would pretty much be impossible to dig anywhere in the woods.

"Is it worth it? All this searching?" I said. "Are you really expecting to find a great pile of treasure?"

She scowled at me. "What do you mean?"

I shrugged. "I dunno. It just sounds a little bit . . . greedy?"

She looked hurt. "No. No, I'm not greedy. I just thought it would be a nice thing to do for Charlotte. That's all. And with you knowing about all sorts of things . . . I thought you might be able to help me. That's why you're here, isn't it?"

Her bright blue eyes shone at me. I felt bad, so I looked away.

"No, I was just trying to catch a chicken, but it's gone now, so I'm going to turn around and go back inside and leave you to it, all right?"

Putting her hands on her hips, she took a step toward me. "Chicken? Why are you catching a chicken? You're not going to kill it and eat it for your lunch, are you?"

"What? No. I just thought, you know, it might need some shelter seeing as it's so cold out here."

Her face softened. To be honest, Kitty looked like the one needing shelter from the winter.

"I think you should go home, Kitty. Someone could freeze to death out here."

She gasped. "You know about the accident then? I knew it! See? You know all sorts of stuff. You even know about the history of this place. I bet you know loads about the Turner-Wrights. You could be so helpful in solving this riddle, Nate. *So* helpful. I don't think I can do it without you."

This was getting ridiculous.

"I don't know anything about an accident. I told you. I have no idea who you are or who your family are, I'm just here on some stupid *holiday* that I didn't want to come on in the first place. You're not the only one with problems, okay?"

I turned to leave.

"My dad always said it was his fault she died," Kitty called after me.

I stopped.

"Who died?" I said. "What are you talking about?"

She tucked her hands into her armpits and sat back on the log.

"You'd better sit down," she said.

I looked up at the swirl of smoke coming out of the cottage chimney and thought about Sam. Was he in there, waiting for me? Ready to show me another weird story? I couldn't cope with any more of that right now. I looked at Kitty, and she sniffed a few times and then took out a tissue, and a huge trumpet noise erupted from her nose. It was nice to see a real person for a bit, even if she was . . . odd. I pulled my coat as tightly around me as I could, and then I sat at the opposite end of the log and listened.

# CHAPTER 12
# KITTY'S STORY

"James, my dad, was born here. His grandfather set up a printing business over eighty years ago, and he bought the house with the money he made. When he died, everything was passed down to the firstborn child, my granddad, and then he passed it on to his own child."

"Your dad?" I said.

"Yes. Dad had a sister named Charlotte who was younger than him."

I quickly interrupted. "And it's her treasure hunt you're trying to solve?"

Kitty nodded. "Yes. As Dad was the eldest, he was destined to run the business after Granddad stopped working. He was next in line to inherit the house and the grounds. His whole future was mapped out for him; he'd be running the business and he'd be living here. Then after him it would all be passed on to his first child, and so on."

I snorted.

"That all sounds a bit Victorian or something," I said. "What if he didn't want to run a business? Or have children, for that matter? Say he wanted to run off and teach surfing or be a musician or something?"

Kitty scowled at me again. "He wouldn't have had a choice; it was just the family tradition."

"And did your dad's sister mind? Knowing that her brother was going to be handed everything while she'd have to go out into the world on her own?"

Kitty edged along the log a little. "I don't think she would have minded. She was really little, though, when it happened."

"When what happened?" I asked, but Kitty ignored me and carried on with her story.

"One of their favorite things to do was put on plays. They only really had each other, remember. James would write the script and they'd both dress up and act it out for the rest of the family in the library."

"The library? You've got a library?!"

Kitty nodded and looked a bit embarrassed. "Yep. We don't really use that part of the house much anymore though. The east wing gets a little . . . chilly."

I opened my mouth to say something about her having a "wing," but I was getting the idea. Kitty's house wasn't just big—it was a stately home. The kind of place I would have visited on a school trip with a gift shop and a tearoom and immaculate lawns that we weren't allowed to run around on. I guess the fact I couldn't even see it from where we were should have given me some idea of the size of the grounds.

"Even though they grew up in an amazing house with acres of land it can be quite lonely living here, but Dad and Charlotte were the best of friends. Charlotte had asthma from an early age, and the doctors said living in a dusty old house didn't help, so they played outside as much as they could. She used to catch lots of colds and chest infections, but Dad always looked out for her and made sure she didn't overdo it."

She stopped for a moment. "Do you have any brothers or sisters?"

I shook my head. It was just me and Mum. Thinking of her, my stomach lurched. It had been nice to forget about everything for a while.

"I don't have any either," she said, gazing back down at the ground.

That must have meant that Kitty was next in line to inherit the house and the business. I wondered how she felt about that.

"It sounds like your dad and Charlotte were both happy living here. So, what happened?"

Kitty took a deep breath. She looked so cold. Then she stood up and did a funny little jog on the spot. "Come on. I'll take you to where it happened."

"Take me to where what happened?"

I stayed on the log while she jumped up and down and beat her arms around herself.

"I'll tell you when we get there. Come on."

I stared back at her, thinking what to do: Did I really want to get involved in this family's past? Shouldn't I just go back to the cottage and lie low, like Mum had told me to?

Kitty stopped flapping her arms. "We'll only be ten minutes. And it's worth seeing, I promise you."

The thought of going back to the empty cottage made my stomach churn. "Okay. But we've got to be quick."

Kitty grinned and I stood up and followed her deeper into the woods.

As we walked, Kitty continued her story:

"When Dad was ten and Charlotte was six there was a party in the house. A magnificent New Year's Eve ball. There was a real band that played music for dancing in the main hall, and there were people dressed up in circus outfits taking trays of drinks and food to the guests. They even had a magician doing card tricks and a troop of fire-eaters on the lawn! The women dressed up in posh gowns and tiaras and the men wore bow ties and there were lights strung up in the trees. The whole place was sparkling!"

Kitty smiled as she thought about it. It was as if she had been there herself.

"Charlotte wore a beautiful ivory dress with shimmering sequins, and James—my dad—had his very own suit and waist-coat. Everyone fussed over them when they saw them. They were the only children there."

"Did you see pictures?" I said.

Kitty nodded. "They hired a photographer. It looked magical." She sighed to herself.

"Everything was going well, but halfway through the evening Dad and Charlotte got bored of all the adults talking and decided to play hide-and-seek. They took turns hiding, but Dad got told off by the cook for going in the kitchen, so they decided to move outside."

Kitty made a little ball with her hands and paused for a moment to blow on her bright red fingers before tucking them deep into her armpits. We came out of the woods into the open, but it didn't get much lighter. I looked for the sun and saw it was really low down. Another half an hour and it would disappear below the horizon altogether.

"Can you tell the story a bit quicker, Kitty? It's going to be dark soon."

Kitty walked toward a tall hedge. "So, everyone was in their ball gowns, drinking champagne and dancing, and Charlotte and Dad sneaked out onto the patio," she continued as we walked beside the hedged wall. "A few guests were outside getting some air, and they said hello to them."

"But if it was New Year's Eve, wasn't it cold?" I said.

"It was freezing! There was even snow on the ground, but Charlotte said they'd have one last game of hide-and-seek and then they'd go back inside to play. She used to boss him around a bit, really, but James, I mean, my dad, always did whatever she said. She told him to count to fifty, and when he shut his eyes she ran here. To the maze."

"Maze?"

I remembered seeing a tall hedge when I had been here with Mum and Dad. It had towered over us, and Mum had run her hand along the thick green leaves.

Kitty stopped and pointed to an overgrown gap in the hedge. It must have been an entrance once upon a time, neatly clipped with an archway over the top. There was a little sign next to it that was covered in frost.

"As you can see, it's really overgrown now. It hasn't been used for years."

I could see it all in my head: Charlotte running across the white lawns in her posh dress. Kitty's dad as a boy standing on the patio covering his eyes as he counted. I shivered.

"The maze was always out of bounds for them, so I don't know why she did it—why she decided that coming here was a good thing to do. It would have been the last place James would have looked, because he knew they weren't allowed there."

I frowned at her. "How do you know all of this?"

Kitty hesitated for a moment. "My dad told me about it, one New Year's Eve. He never mentioned it again."

I wasn't sure how much he'd told her or how much Kitty was making up as she went along, but either way, she was pretty impressive as a storyteller. I wanted to know what happened next, but she stayed silent for so long I didn't think she was going to tell me, and then she suddenly ducked into the maze. The branches shuddered and closed behind her. It was as if they'd swallowed her up.

"Kitty? Kitty, don't mess around," I called through the entrance. There was no reply. I pushed a few branches out of the way and peered inside. The maze was so overgrown there was barely any room to get through. I edged forward a pace.

"Kitty? Where are you?"

I stopped to listen, to see if I could hear her rustling about, but there was nothing.

"Kitty! Don't mess around, okay?"

A hand suddenly appeared through the greenery. I gasped, and then Kitty's face appeared, her eyes glistening white in the gloom.

"Don't ever, ever do that again, okay?" I shouted with my hand at my chest. My heart was doing that mad fluttering again. I'd thought it was Gary. I'd thought he'd found me.

"I'm sorry. I was joking, that's all. I didn't mean to scare you."

I glared at her. "Well, you did. Okay? Feel better now?"

She looked quite upset. "I'm really sorry."

I stuffed my hands into my pockets.

"So . . . what happened then?" I asked, scuffing my foot on the ground. "What happened to Charlotte?"

I looked down the dark corridor, but it was so thick with branches I couldn't see much.

Kitty's eyes widened as she got back to her story. This time she spoke in whispers.

"James counted to fifty and then he called out, into the cold night air, 'Coming, ready or not!' He searched all their usual places, the rose beds, the topiary garden, behind all of the statues, but she was nowhere to be seen. It was nearly midnight and all of the guests piled out onto the patio, ready to count down to the start of the new year."

I was shivering so much my teeth chattered together. This story was chilling me to the bone, but I wanted to know what happened next. What happened to Charlotte.

"The crowd was chanting: 'Eight! Seven! Six! Five!' James ran around the adults, trying to find his mum and dad, but there were so many people he couldn't spot them. He tried to get the grown-ups' attention, tugging on their arms and their sleeves. 'Charlotte's missing! I can't find her! You've got to help!' he shouted at them, but he couldn't make them listen. 'Four! Three! Two! One! Happy New Year!' Everyone began singing 'Auld Lang Syne' and hugging and kissing one another, but eventually a man saw that James was crying. James told him that he didn't know where his sister was and word quickly spread around. Everyone stopped celebrating and began to search."

She shook her head and lowered her eyes.

"Someone found her in the middle of the maze."

"Oh," I said. "That's so sad."

Kitty nodded. "She must have gotten lost. The doctors said that the cold weather and panic brought on an asthma attack. And . . . she . . . she died."

"How terrible," I said. "Your dad must have felt awful."

Kitty nodded. She pointed toward the thick branches. "Do you want to go and see if we can find where they found her?"

I shook my head. That was the last thing I wanted to do. Kitty's story had made me feel a bit ill.

"I'd better be getting back. My parents will be worried," I said, and I pushed my way back out into the open, Kitty following. I was so cold I couldn't feel my feet, and I tried to wiggle my toes as I walked but they hurt.

"This treasure hunt you're trying to solve," I said. "I'm guessing James and Charlotte never solved it . . . because she died?"

She nodded.

"They were planning to, but then the accident happened and it was all forgotten about. I really want to solve it now. Especially as it was for Charlotte. I often wonder what treasure William would have left for her. It would be a nice thing to do in her memory, don't you think?"

We were quiet for a moment, and I thought about everything she'd said. It was a relief to put my problems out of my mind for a bit.

We got back to the woods, and I stopped and turned to face her.

"Kitty? You know the riddle you're trying to solve? It's a yew tree. The next clue is hidden near a yew tree."

She gasped. "Wh-What?"

The delighted shock on her face made me smile. "It says it in the riddle: 'I'm a thousand years old, yet still strong as lead.' Yew trees can live for thousands of years, and their wood is really strong. And you know it's a tree from the description about the roots, but the biggest clue is in the line: 'I'm symbolic of life, yet watch over the dead.' Yews are seen as symbols of everlasting life because they stay green all year-round, and they can often be found in churchyards, so that's why he's put that about 'watching over the dead.' I read it in a book. All you need to do is find an ancient-looking tree that is still green and is planted in a churchyard."

Kitty's mouth was dangling open. The silence made me feel a bit awkward.

"Thank you! Do you know how long I've been trying to solve this clue? Ages and ages! And then you come along and solve it straight away! You're amazing."

I smiled and my cheeks went a bit warm. Kitty was quite sweet when she wanted to be. "Are there any churches nearby?"

Kitty gathered her things together and threw her satchel over a shoulder. "There's no need to even go out of the grounds. I know *exactly* where he means, and I'm going over there right now. You coming?"

She stood there with her shovel in one hand. It felt good to feel wanted. And being called *amazing*—that was pretty cool too. I took a look at the sky blinking through the waving tops of the trees. It was going to get dark really, really soon.

"Okay, but we've got to be quick," I said.

# CHAPTER 13

# THE YEW TREE

We walked through the woods to the other side, and when we came out I saw that the sky was a dark pink and looked heavy with snow. And it suddenly felt much, much colder.

"Where are we going exactly?" I said as Kitty turned left and headed down a hill. I was struggling to keep up with her.

"There's an old family chapel down in the valley. I haven't been there in *years*. In fact, I completely forgot there was one."

I burst out laughing. "How can you forget you've got a chapel? Kitty, you're not of this world!"

She looked around and her face dropped. I turned to see what had made her frown and saw the corner of a building. It must have been her house. The brickwork was gray and dark, but I could only see a fraction of it; the rest of the house was hidden by tall trees.

"Is that your home?" I asked.

She nodded and turned away quickly. "Come on, the chapel is over there. Look!"

Kitty pointed. Nestling in the dip of the hill was a little brown church. It was surrounded by an old stone wall that had crumbled in places.

I jogged to catch up with her. I remembered now that Mum had said the big house had its own chapel. She'd said it when we were hitting the rug with our sticks in the garden; she'd said we'd seen it when we'd stayed before.

It was starting to sleet, and the cold, freezing rain hit my face like pinpricks.

Kitty came to a break in the wall and clambered over the pile of stones. I looked around and saw a huge tree with a trunk the color of hot chocolate. Its roots were twisted and gnarled and its canopy of green looked like a giant umbrella.

"There it is," I said. "That's your yew."

Kitty headed straight toward it. "These roots are worse than the ones in the wood. I'm never going to be able to dig here."

I walked around the tree, trying not to twist my ankle in the tangled wood. "Maybe it's not buried at all. We should look in the gaps and see if he's hidden something in there. Be careful though, it might look nice, but this tree is really poisonous."

I looked in all the crevices.

"It might not even be here anymore, Kitty. It might have just rotted away."

Kitty scowled. "Of course it's still here. I'll start looking around this side."

I crouched down and peered into all the little holes that the yew tree's roots had created. I don't think I'd ever been this close to one before. It really was very impressive. Kitty was around the other side of the tree, and the trunk was so wide I couldn't even see her.

"Anything?" I called.

"No . . . nothing. Wait. Hold on—I think there's something . . ."

I scrambled around the side just as she was poking a stick into a hole. She scraped at it a few times, and then finally something appeared. It was a little wooden box. She dropped the stick and grabbed it.

"I don't believe it! We've found it! Oh . . ."

She opened the box and a piece of paper fell onto the ground, which she picked up, smoothed out, and read:

Clue 2

THINK OF AN I,

THEN THINK OF AN H.

THEN UNLOCK THE DOOR

TO A COLD, FROZEN PLACE.

She looked at me. "Any ideas?"

I shrugged. "No. But I think I'm going to go back now. My parents will be wondering where I am."

I wasn't comfortable being out when Mum could arrive at any moment. I turned and walked back the way we'd come and Kitty followed, still holding the clue in her hand.

"Search for an *I* and an *H*. What do you think that means? Shall we have a look in William's cottage? Maybe it's something to do with a book."

I grunted as I scrambled over the slippery, broken wall.

"Slow down, Nate. You're going too fast," she said as she tried to keep up with me. "What's the hurry? We need to talk about the clue."

I ignored her and strode toward the woods, but she quickened her step and jogged alongside me.

"We need to think where we should look next. Do you have any ideas?"

I stopped when I got to the trees. "No, but good luck with it all anyway. I'm sure you'll work it out," I said, and I began to jog away.

"Shall we check the cottage now?" she asked, catching up with me. "It could be in there. I really think we should check in the books."

I stopped and turned toward her. "Look. I think what you're doing with trying to solve this riddle is really great and all that, but I must get back. On my own."

Kitty frowned at me, and then her face softened as she looked at something past my ear. "Oh look! Your parents are here!"

I couldn't see properly through the trees, but I could definitely hear something. It sounded like a car traveling really slowly. Tires were scrunching along the frozen dirt track. Mum was back! I began to run.

"I'll come back tomorrow at ten!" Kitty shouted as I disappeared through the iron gate and into the cottage garden.

# CHAPTER 14

# HIDING

There was a *Freaky Things* fact that I knew quite well, and I was remembering it in my head while I hid behind the sofa, trying to ignore the stranger banging on the front door.

*It's your birthday and you live in a remote village in the Himalayas! So . . . how do you receive your birthday cards? Why, by monkey, of course! A rhesus macaque named Mike delivers the mail to the villagers of Konapanthi each day, carrying the letters and parcels in a custom-designed monkey backpack that allows him to race across the mountains, ensuring that the mail is always on time! How about that for an a-monkey-mazing mailman!!!!!*

As I recited the fact in my head, the pounding on the front door continued—and it definitely wasn't Mum. It was somebody in a red van; I'd seen it as I ran through the garden, and I'd managed to get in through the kitchen door before they spotted me. Maybe Gary had been following us after all and he was just waiting for the right time to make his move? Maybe he'd driven a red van so we didn't spot his car? I heard the crunch of footsteps on the gravel and I waited for a car engine to start back up again, but instead there was knocking on the window. Really hard.

*Bang, bang, bang!*

They weren't giving up.

I shut my eyes tight as I thought about the Himalayan monkey, scampering across the rocks to make sure some little kid got their birthday cards on time. The photograph in the book was of a monkey wearing a cap with the word *mailman* on the top. Would the people of the Himalayas use the word *mailman*? Wouldn't they use a word from their own language? The more I thought about it, the more I suspected that Mum may have been right all along. Maybe the book was rubbish after all.

There were more footsteps, and I suddenly remembered that the kitchen door was unlocked. All they had to do was walk around the side, open the door, and come straight in. I looked toward the kitchen. Maybe I could crawl across the floor, get to the kitchen, then quickly bolt the door? But the footsteps had gone back to the front door and there was a squeaking sound as they tried the mailbox, but it just gave a pathetic thud. And then:

*Bang, bang, bang!*

They pounded on the door with a fist again.

"Psssst! Who are we hiding from?"

I jumped. Sam had appeared beside me, also sitting on the floor, also hugging his knees.

"I think it might be Gary. I think he's found us," I whispered back.

*Bang, bang, bang!*

I began to shake.

"I'm sure it's not him. How could he know where you are? He doesn't know about this place, and you know yourself that no one was following you."

I nodded. He was right, but I still flinched when the knocking started again.

"Sam, what are we going to do?" I said. "They might come around the back. I left the kitchen door unlocked."

There was a creak of the mailbox opening again and then a dull thud as it sprang shut. It sounded like they'd left something.

"Shhhhh, it sounds like they're going," said Sam. "Listen."

There were more footsteps and then the sound of a car door opening and slamming shut. An engine turned on and I listened as it slowly reversed off the driveway and sped up as it trundled toward the dirt track. I squeezed my eyes together, trying not to cry. I wanted it to have been Mum so much. Where was she? Why wasn't she coming back for me? I had thought of a reason—a horrible reason with sharp edges—for why she might not be here, but I pushed it out of my mind.

"Come on!" said Sam, jumping up.

"Hold on, shouldn't we wait for a minute?" I said. "We should definitely wait for a bit and make sure he's gone."

The boy with the yellow glow laughed. "Come on. You don't really think it's Gary, do you? How on earth do you think he found you? Do you think he had a tracker on your car or something?"

I stayed still, hugging my knees. Maybe he had. Maybe he knew Mum had rented out that car and hidden a tracker in the trunk without her knowing. He'd not been following us, but he knew where we were from the tracking device. Maybe he'd found Mum and that's why she hadn't come back and now he was coming to get me. I started to cry.

"Hey, no need for tears," said Sam, his face full of concern. "You stay here and I'll go and check that the coast is clear. Okay?"

He gave me a smile and ran to the front door while I waited behind the sofa. It felt like he was quiet for ages, but then:

"Nate! Come and see this!"

My heart plummeted. Whatever it was, it was going to be bad news, I just knew it. I stood up and slowly made my way to the front door.

"Look!" said Sam, a big grin on his face. On the mat by his feet was a small red-and-white card with something scribbled on it. I picked it up and read:

## Your parcel has been left:
BEHIND THE PLANT POT.

I laughed. It hadn't been Gary knocking after all. It must have been a delivery person. There was no tracker after all. Gary had no idea where I was. I felt the panic drain away down my body. Sam was jumping around beside me.

"Cool! It must be outside. Go and see what it is, Nate."

I wondered who would be sending a parcel to an empty cottage. I pulled the door open and squeezed outside while Sam waited, jiggling on the spot like an excited three-year-old. Around the side, where Mum had gone searching for the door key, was a large brown plant pot. Whatever had been growing in it must have died and rotted away years ago, and stuffed behind it was a brown padded envelope. I pulled it out and went back indoors, shoving the door shut with my shoulder.

"What is it? What is it? Open it!" said Sam, practically hysterical with excitement.

I sat at the dining table and looked at the front. It was addressed to *Mr. W. Blakelore.*

"That must be William. The gardener who lived here. Who would have sent him something? He died months ago."

"Just open it!" said Sam.

I felt the flat parcel all over and gave it a shake, but it didn't rattle. And there was no return address on the back. I put my finger into the little gap at the edge of the opening and began to pull it across, but then I stopped and turned the parcel over and stared at the address.

Sam waved his hands in my face. "Why have you stopped? Come on!"

I shook my head. "No. It's not my name on the front, so it's not mine to open."

Sam looked utterly baffled. "What?! But there's no one here to know. Just do it!"

I put the parcel on the table. "Gary used to open Mum's mail. She said it was *her* name on the envelope, so it should only be opened by her. She was really brave and stood up to him, then."

Mum had told me to go to my room at that point and I had lain on my bed and read my *Freaky Things* book while they argued downstairs. I looked up at Sam.

"It's not addressed to me, so I'm not going to open it," I said, and I threw the parcel back onto the table and went into the kitchen.

# CHAPTER 15
# GARY

I sorted the food in the kitchen into three piles: would eat, would eat if desperate, would not eat in a million years.

Sam was watching me.

"Was Gary always scary?" he suddenly asked.

I stopped what I was doing for a moment and shook my head, and then I carried on moving the cans into their piles.

"So, do you remember when it all started? When things went bad?"

"Yep," I said. Still sorting through the cans.

Sam took a step closer, and I stopped what I was doing. My legs were beginning to tremble, and I slowly sat down on the kitchen floor and leaned against a cupboard door.

"It might be good, you know," said Sam. "To talk about it?"

I took a breath and rested my head against the cold cabinet door as Sam sat down beside me, and then I told him what had happened.

---

When I was nine, we had a World History Day at school. We all had to go in dressed as someone from the past, and the week beforehand we were all talking about who we were going to be. David Fletcher was going to stick a pillow under his shirt, put on a red beard, and go as King Henry VIII, and Amelia Worrell said she was going to wear a black wig and eyeliner and go as Cleopatra. When it came to my turn I said it was a secret, but the truth was, I didn't actually know. Mum had been making an outfit for me, and she wanted it to be a surprise.

She worked in the dining room in the evenings, smuggling in sheets of cardboard, newspapers, and glue. Gary had been living with us for about a year back then, and he wasn't impressed.

"What are you doing in there all this time?" he said, banging on the door for the third evening running.

"Don't come in! I don't want to spoil the surprise," called Mum.

Gary huffed and raised his eyes at me, and I'd given him a weak smile as he went back to his TV program in the front room. I didn't like it when Mum gave me too much attention. I don't know why, but it made me feel nervous. I didn't think Gary liked it.

The evening before World History Day, Mum walked into the front room with a bundle of clothes. We were going to find out what she'd been spending all her time on. She was so excited, her eyes wide.

"Right. Nate, first you need to put this on, and then I'll show you the rest, okay?"

She passed me a white shirt and tie, a navy suit with gold braiding on each sleeve, and a navy-and-white cap. I hesitated as I stood with the clothes folded over my arms. Gary was sitting on the sofa looking at something on his phone, his legs dangling over the arm, his shoes still on. Mum had asked him not to wear them indoors, but he never listened.

"Go on then, Nate! Run to your room and put it on!" said Mum again.

I quickly went upstairs and threw the clothes on my bed. I could tell it was some type of uniform; she must have found a small suit and sewn the gold bands onto the sleeves herself. I put the shirt, jacket, trousers, and cap on but left the tie off. Mum would have to help me with that one.

When I walked into the front room, Mum jumped up and clapped her hands.

"Look at you! You're a proper little captain! Isn't he, Gary?"

Gary snorted without looking up.

"It's great, Mum," I said. "But . . . who am I meant to be?"

Gary snickered again and said something under his breath. I wished he'd gone out. I just wanted Mum to enjoy showing me what she'd made without him making stupid noises.

"Wait there, I'll go and get the best bit," said Mum and she disappeared off into the dining room.

"You know you don't have to wear what she tells you," said Gary, staring at me with his piercing blue eyes. "It's fine to say no if you feel like an idiot."

He had a smile on his face like he was trying to be kind. I looked down at the costume. I didn't feel like an idiot.

"You don't want the other kids to start picking on you because you look like a jerk, do you?"

Mum came in and he quickly looked back down at his phone.

"Ta-daaaa!" she said. "Well, what do you think?"

She was carrying a large papier-mâché ship. It was painted dark gray, and along the side was written "RMS *TITANIC*" in black ink. I was gobsmacked. She put it down on the carpet. I could see the middle had a space cut out where I could stand, and she'd attached two red suspenders that would hook up over my shoulders. My mouth dropped. It was simply the best costume I'd ever seen in my whole life.

"Wow!" I said. "You've made the *Titanic*! You've actually made the *Titanic*!"

Mum laughed and clapped her hands together again. Her eyes looked a bit watery. "I know! Let's get it on you then. Just step in, and I'll lift it up for you."

I climbed carefully into the middle of the ship, and Mum put the red suspenders on my shoulders. I was going to school dressed as the *Titanic*, and this was the best thing in the whole world.

"It's two costumes in one, really, isn't it, Mum? I'm the captain of the *Titanic*, and I'm the actual *Titanic*. It's brilliant!"

Mum grinned as I walked around the living room, being careful not to knock into anything. Gary had his arms folded and was watching silently.

"So, you're quite happy sending your son to school dressed like that, are you?"

Mum's face dropped, but then she forced a smile. "Don't be silly, Gary. He looks fantastic! Look at him! He's bound to win a best costume prize, don't you think?"

Gary rubbed his chin, and I heard the scratch of his stubble against his hand. "Do they give out a prize for the most ridiculous outfit then?"

Mum and I stood there in silence. He got up, walked out of the room, and stomped his way upstairs. Mum flinched when the bathroom door slammed.

"Don't you go taking any notice of him, will you, Nate? You look great. Let's get this off and we'll leave it in the dining room, ready for tomorrow, okay?"

She helped me take the suspenders off, and once I was out of the ship I gave her a big hug.

"Thanks, Mum. It's really, really brilliant," I said.

I went to bed that night listening to a distant rumble of thunder as Mum and Gary talked in the bedroom next door. I couldn't hear what they were saying, but Gary kept doing that laugh he does—the one where you're not sure if it's real or not. Mum's voice was going quiet then getting louder, and I knew she must be walking up and down the room. I wasn't sure why, but something about the *Titanic* outfit had upset Gary, and I could sense that Mum was trying to make things all right again. I heard his sickening laugh one more time and then their bedroom door opened and closed and someone went downstairs.

I tried to ignore the knotted feeling in my tummy. Gary had changed in the last few months, but I was hoping it was just my imagination. After all, there'd been plenty of days when he'd been really, really nice. He'd taken me to the movies only last week and he'd made me laugh so much that lemonade had shot out of my nose. That was a great day. I was just a bit worried that the good days were becoming rare and we were seeing a lot more of not-so-nice Gary.

I stuffed my arm under my mattress and pulled out the secret string of lights from my little light jar that used to sit on the shelf. I clicked them on under the duvet and watched the bulbs twinkle in the darkness.

The next morning, when I came down for breakfast, Mum was in the kitchen with her back to me, fiddling with something on the table. It was something gray.

"Mum? What's happened?" I asked. "What's happened to the *Titanic*?!"

Mum jumped. "Nate! Oh, you gave me a shock. I didn't hear you."

I could see that she'd been crying, as her eyes were red, but she quickly turned away so that I couldn't look at her. On the table was my ship, but it didn't look like a ship any more. It was a shapeless lump of wet cardboard. She was trying to straighten the sides up, but every time she let go, the boat slumped back down again.

"Why's it like that?" I said, close to tears. "Why is it all floppy? It's ruined!"

Mum brushed her hair away from her face. "It got a bit wet in the rain last night. I'm sure we can dry it out. I'll get my hairdryer and we'll have a go, okay? It's going to be fine."

It didn't look fine. It looked like a pile of wet cardboard, and the gray paint had run so I could see the bold print underneath saying BAKED BEANS. Then I saw the captain's suit was hanging over the radiator, also soaked. The drips had made a wet puddle on the tiled floor.

"How did it get in the rain? You put it in the dining room! Who put it in the rain?!"

Just then Gary appeared in the doorway. He was dressed in his suit, ready for work, and he stood there with a smirk on his face.

"Something wrong?" he said, walking to the fridge and getting out some milk. Mum and I both watched him as he opened the carton of milk and drank from the spout. I felt sick.

"Did you put my ship in the rain?" I asked, taking a small step toward him, but Mum pressed her hand on my arm.

Gary finished drinking the milk and then wiped the white mustache away from his lips. He was about to say something when Mum butted in.

"I put it outside. I wanted to make sure the paint was properly dry before this morning, and I didn't know it was going to rain."

I looked at Mum as she fixed eyes with Gary. I knew she was lying. I couldn't believe she was sticking up for him.

"No, you didn't. He did it. You wouldn't have worked so hard on something only to let it get ruined. It was raining before I went to bed last night, and there's no way you would have put it outside in that. Or the suit!"

Gary closed the fridge and slowly walked around the kitchen as if he was looking for something. He wasn't really doing anything, but his whole body was rigid and his movements were so exact it didn't feel right. I was terrified. Any second now he was going to explode. Any second now he would do something.

He took a banana off the top of the fruit bowl.

"I'm late for work," he said, staring at Mum before turning to me. "Enjoy your dress-up day, won't you, Nate? I'm sure you'll have a lot of fun. Oh, and, Fiona? Could you clean this up for me?"

Mum looked at him, puzzled.

"Clean what up?" she said, her arms hugging herself.

"This," said Gary.

He picked up the glass fruit bowl, held it at chest height, and dropped it onto the kitchen floor, where it smashed into a million pieces.

My legs went weak, and I felt like I was going to fall to the floor with the shock. I held on to the table, my heart pounding as I watched Gary staring at Mum. She was frozen, stunned by what had just happened.

"I'll be late tonight," he said. "Don't bother making me any dinner." And then, as if he'd just behaved perfectly normally, he turned and walked out the front door.

I was late for school that morning. It took us an hour to sweep up the glass and pieces of fruit, and then we realized that Mum's ankle was bleeding where a sharp piece must have hit her.

I stuffed the wet, ruined cardboard *Titanic* into a black garbage bag while Mum dabbed at her leg with a tissue. She hadn't said anything about what had happened. Was she going to pretend everything was okay?

I went to school dressed in a black sweater and pants, and Mum smudged some black makeup across my cheeks and ruffled up my hair.

"There. You are a perfect little chimney sweep."

"But that's stupid!" I said. "I'm supposed to be a famous person. There weren't any famous chimney sweeps!"

Mum glared at me.

"I'm doing my best, Nate, okay?" And then she turned her back on me.

At school, no one knew who I was, and after the fifteenth person asked me, I lost it.

"Just forget it, okay? I'm nobody! Just leave me alone."

I spent the rest of the day being left alone, which was exactly the way I wanted it.

# CHAPTER 16

# SEARCHING THE COTTAGE

I sat alone at the dining table and ate some canned pineapple chunks followed by cold custard, which were both in my "would eat" pile. It was really dark outside, so as soon as I finished, I quickly went into every room in the cottage and turned on all the lights and lamps. My dinner sloshed around in my stomach as I went, and I felt a bit sick. Then I sat on the sofa and flicked through my book.

*Do you know what King Charles II's favorite food was? Boar's head burgers? Swan soup? No! It was ice cream! Yes, that cheeky, curly haired monarch used to get through EIGHT scoops a day. Ice-Cream Cone Crazy! But how did they make ice cream all those hundreds of years ago with no electricity? With no ice-cream maker? Well, this lucky king had an ice house in his back garden—an underground construction made of bricks that was packed with snow and ice that the servants collected during wintertime. This ice house would stay chilly all year-round and was the perfect place to store the king's ice cream. It was a right royal refrigerator!*

I stared at the hand-drawn picture of the curly-haired king holding an ice cream the size of a tennis racket. His eyes were wide, the crown on his head almost falling off as his teeth sank into the creamy swirl.

"Mum was right. This book is stupid," I said to myself as I threw it on the living room floor. "How can anyone expect to be able to store snow and ice through the summer? It's ridiculous! I don't know who wrote that book, but they are well and truly deluded."

I was talking out loud in the hope that Sam would turn up to keep me company, but there was no sign of him. I got up and took my dinner bowls to the kitchen and rinsed them under the tap.

When I got back to the living room, Sam was sitting at the table turning my blue flashlight on and off. I was pleased to see him, but really I wanted my mum. I wanted her here now, singing in the kitchen and making me scrambled eggs. But she wasn't. There was just a glowing yellow boy who seemed to be able to appear whenever he wanted. I took a deep breath.

"Can you put my flashlight down, please, Sam? You'll wear the battery out," I said as I walked past him.

"What's your problem with the dark, Nate?" he said, still flicking the flashlight on and off.

I ignored him and went over to try and sort the fire out. I'd let it die down too much, and now it was so cold I was breathing puffs of white air. I blew on my fingers to try to warm them up.

"What happened, Nate? Tell me."

I shot him a look, then went back to raking the ash in the fire. I didn't want to talk about it. Not right now.

"So, are you going to help Kitty?" asked Sam.

"No," I said as I carefully relit the fire.

"You know, it might be fun," said Sam. "I bet there're all sorts of interesting things hidden about this place, don't you? I mean, look at all this stuff!"

Sam waved his hand toward the mantelpiece and the collection of bric-a-brac that covered every surface in the room.

"And she did think that you were pretty wonderful for solving that first clue. I bet you could solve the next one just like that!" He snapped his fingers.

He was right. I had solved the first clue pretty easily, but the new one seemed more cryptic. *Think of an I, then think of an H* was puzzling me. Sam was watching me.

"*And* it would give you something to do . . ." he said.

He was right. I didn't actually have anything to do, and I wasn't in the mood for puzzles, reading any more of my book, or my stupid magic ball.

"I think . . ." I said. "I think maybe I'll have a poke around the cottage and see if I can find anything."

I shot a look at Sam, who was smiling and glowing like he was the sun or something.

I started with the mantelpiece above the wood stove. Ornaments and vases had been jammed together into every possible space. I searched through a china pot that was crammed full of pens and blunt pencils but found nothing interesting. I picked up each of the ornaments, giving them a shake to see if anything had been hidden inside, but I only found lots of dust and the odd dead fly. In between the statues and figures were some old receipts and a few unused stamps that had been torn off envelopes. I pushed the wooden clock to one side and the bell inside gave a gentle *bong*, and then I checked behind the circular mirror above the fire, just in case there was a hidden safe with a black dial like you saw in spy movies, but it was just a bare wall.

The kitchen cupboards didn't hold any secrets, though I found some packets of dried tomato soup that I put in the "would eat" pile.

Upstairs there was nothing in the bathroom, and just some old holey sweaters in the bottom of the wardrobe in my room.

Mum's room was the last place left to look.

I sat on her bed for a bit. I hadn't noticed before, but it had been neatly made with the covers smoothed down and tightly tucked in after her one night of sleep. She never made her bed at home, unless you counted throwing the duvet up over the pillow. Here it looked like she'd really taken her time to make it nice. Her small bag was on the floor where I'd left it with my present waiting inside. I felt sick. Where was she? The bad thought came back into my head again, and I pushed it away.

"You're not doing a great job of treasure hunting just sitting there, are you?"

Sam appeared in the doorway, and I sprang up as he walked in.

"Come on, Nate. You can do this—I know you can. Just think. *I* and *H*. What could that mean?"

"I'm trying, okay?" I said, but my mind was blank.

I took a look under the bed and then tugged on the drawers in the big, heavy chest. The top one had a black comb, a few chess pieces, and an empty picture frame rattling around inside. The second was full of smelly old clothes, and in the bottom one there were lots of yellowing newspapers. Underneath the papers was a brown folder labeled *House and Grounds: Maps/Plans*. Inside were some typed letters dating from the 1970s that appeared to be about some kind of building application. There was a map of the local area and a large, folded piece of paper that showed the plans of Kitty's house and garden. I laid it out on the floor.

"Wow," I said. "It's huge."

The house was drawn in sharp pencil and appeared to have three floors and a lot of rooms. Each room had a fancy name, such as the Grand Study, Children's Day Nursery, Brontë Reading Room, and the Music Chamber.

Sam peered over my shoulder. "Anything?"

"Nothing," I said. I folded the plans carefully and put them back.

I sat on the sofa downstairs and watched the light of the fire flicker against the wall. Every few minutes I looked up at the darkness outside, just in case Mum's car lights appeared. I'd have to go to bed soon, but the thought of that made me feel anxious. Where was she? Would I have to stay here on my own forever? Had something terrible happened to her?

I stared at the figurines lined up along the mantelpiece. There was a man dressed in a fancy blue-and-white suit who was tipping his hat toward a girl who looked away shyly under a parasol. Two spaniels with beady eyes sat side by side; their heads looked too big for their bodies and they had their noses in the air. Sam was sitting in the armchair looking through my *Freaky Things* book. He kept snickering every now and then.

"Did you see this? This story about Charles the Second and the ice cream? How ridiculous. As if ice houses existed. Do they think we are idiots? Ha. And this one about the monkey! I've never read so much rubbish before . . ."

I held my breath for a moment. "Whoa, hold on a minute. What did you just say?"

Sam looked up at me over the book. "The story about the monkey? I was just saying what . . ."

"No, no, no . . . before then. About Charles the Second. Let me take a look."

I jumped up and grabbed the book from him and found the right page. I quickly skimmed through the lines, and there it was.

"That's it! *I* and *H*! It's an ice house! The next clue is hidden in the ice house! It's obvious if you think about it. The final line in the clue said, 'Then unlock the door to a cold, frozen place.' An ice house! Of course it is."

I sat back on the sofa feeling pretty pleased with myself. Sam was beaming at me, his whole outline glowing yellow.

"See? I knew you could do it! I just knew it," he said.

But then my smile fell as I looked at the picture in the book in my lap. There was Charles II with his silly, giant ice cream, but in the corner of the page was a photograph of a real ice house. A redbrick arched entrance had been dug into the side of a hill, and inside it looked very, very dark.

"You should get some sleep," said Sam.

I picked up my book and Mrs. Ellie-Fant and walked to the stairs.

"Where is she, Sam? Where's my mum?"

Sam looked at me sadly, and then his colors faded until he disappeared. I was all alone once more.

# CHAPTER 17
# KITTY KNOCKS

I flicked through my book the next morning as I lay in bed.

*Do you know how the hot dog was invented? In 1876 a lady named Eloise Gibson was sitting eating a salami roll on an exceptionally warm day in Central Park, when Stanley Robinson walked by with his Jack Russell terrier, Poochy. The little dog stopped and sniffed at Eloise's ankle, who let out a yelp and threw her salami roll up into the air!*

*"Oh gee, I'm real sorry," said Stanley. "Poochy just wanted to say howdy to you!"*

*Eloise looked down at her lunch, which was now sitting on the little dog's back. "If I were you, sir, I'd take your animal somewhere cooler. He is clearly one hot dog!"*

*Stanley looked at the woman.*

*Looked at his dog.*

*And that, dear readers, was a eureka moment! Stanley Robinson went on to invent the hot dog and became a zillionaire . . .*

I'd seen a program on TV once that talked about the history of the hot dog, and I'm sure it had something to do with Germany and dachshunds, not Jack Russells. I lay there for a moment, listening to the sounds of the creaky old cottage. Hoping that somehow

Mum had come back in the middle of the night and I hadn't heard her. But all I could hear were the rustling of the trees outside and a robin singing as if his life depended on it.

"Nate! Nate? Are you there?"

I sat bolt upright. Mum? Was that Mum? I jumped out of bed. Someone was downstairs.

"We agreed ten o'clock! Hello?"

My stomach dropped as I recognized the voice. It wasn't Mum at all; it was Kitty. Wrapping the cowboy duvet around my shoulders, I headed down.

When I opened the living room door she was already inside, wearing her blue woolly hat with her brown satchel across her chest. I thought I'd locked the front door, and I was angry with myself for forgetting. Anyone could have come in during the night.

"Ah, you're up! Well, sort of. Are you ill?"

I shook my head. It wasn't Mum. She still wasn't back. I felt my stomach knot again. "No, I just hadn't seen the time. Did you . . . Did you just let yourself in?"

I couldn't quite believe she'd done that. She opened her mouth but then shrugged. "I was cold. So, are you going to get ready then or what? We still have the next clue to solve."

I remembered I'd already guessed the answer, and I grinned at her.

"Wait right there!" I said, and I ran upstairs to get dressed. I was so cold I grabbed a sweater from the wardrobe in my room, trying to ignore the dusty smell. The sleeves were far too long, and

I folded them up my arms the best I could. I also took the folder from the bottom drawer, the one with the plans and map of the house and grounds.

The bathroom was so cold there was a thin layer of ice on the inside of the window, and I scratched a tiny circle in it with my fingernail as I brushed my teeth. I really needed to take a shower, but hopefully the layers of clothes would hide any smell.

When I got back downstairs Kitty was inspecting the row of ornaments on the mantelpiece. "Are your parents out again?"

I rubbed the top of my head. "They're . . . erm, they're out getting samples of carpets and stuff. They won't be back for hours, I would imagine. My parents are pretty busy people."

Kitty nodded at me but didn't say anything as she walked over to the window and looked out onto the driveway. "They must have left really early. There's no sign of a car being there."

It had snowed in the night and there was a light dusting covering everything, including the driveway. If I'd been telling the truth, there should be a patch of snow-free ground where the car had been.

I opened my mouth but I literally couldn't think of anything to say, so I just shut it again. My stomach gave a loud growl that sounded a bit like a rumble of distant thunder.

"Oh, I brought you something," said Kitty, rummaging in her brown satchel. She passed me a brown paper bag. "It's a muffin. You like butterscotch, don't you? I usually have chocolate chip, but I thought I'd give these a try."

I opened the bag and a smell of cinnamon, toasted marshmallows, and warm bakeries wafted up my nose. Inside was the most amazing-looking muffin I'd ever seen. I pulled it out and took a huge bite. It was still warm and it tasted so good it brought tears to my eyes.

"Kitty . . . this is . . . wow . . ." I said, stuffing another mouthful in.

She smiled. "Oh wow, you must be really hungry."

I'd eaten the whole thing. I grinned and went to brush the crumbs off the smelly sweater, but I must have eaten it so quickly there weren't any. I realized then that there was a great big hole in the front by the hem, but Kitty didn't seem to notice.

"What's your favorite type of scone, fruit or cheese?" she said, blinking her eyelashes at me.

"Erm. Cheese, perhaps? I think. Or fruit. I don't really mind."

I stared at her. Was there a reason she was keen to give me food? Had she realized that everything I had been telling her was a complete lie? That I was on my own?

"But there's no need to bring anything else over, if that's why you're asking," I said quickly. "I think we might be leaving later today. My parents have an appointment about another development, you see . . . in London. So . . . you know, I might be gone."

She nodded but I could tell she didn't believe a word of it. Before she could ask me any more questions, I jumped in with my news. "I think I solved the riddle last night."

Kitty's eyes lit up, dazzling blue.

I opened the brown folder and took out the plans of the house and grounds. I made some space on the table and spread the paper out. "This is your house, isn't it? And the grounds?"

Kitty gasped. "Wow! This is amazing. I've never seen a map of the house before."

I pointed at some of the rooms. "Look, all the rooms have names. The French Room, the Breakfast Room, the Floral Bedroom."

Kitty nodded. "Yes, they do! Ah, I like your thinking!" She quickly scanned them. "But there's nothing with the letters *I* and *H*," she said.

"No," I said, unfolding the plans a little more so that all of the grounds could be seen. I was hoping it would be on there somewhere, and I traced my finger along the pathways on the grounds, past the stables and down a hill, and then tapped hard on the table.

"There! *That* is an ice house."

Next to a faint circle was a little arrow, and a label in fancy scroll next to it read *Ice house*.

Kitty frowned as she stared at the map. "An ice house . . . Of course. I knew it, Nate! I knew you'd be the one to solve all of these clues. Brilliant! But what's it for?"

"Wait here," I said and I ran upstairs and grabbed my *Freaky Things* book, then came back down and showed her the bit about ice houses.

"This book does exaggerate a bit, but I think most of the things are based on truth. Ice houses *do* exist on the grounds of big houses. They used to pack them full of snow and ice and use them to preserve food throughout the year. And that is where you'll find your next clue." I shut the book with a satisfying smack.

Kitty beamed at me. "Of course! They used to use the ice house as a den, apparently. Dad hung up little lanterns, and they put some old chairs in there. William would have definitely wanted to hide something there."

Her face was so happy I couldn't help but smile back.

"I'm so pleased you've decided to help me with this, Nate. I wasn't sure . . . you know . . . if you were up for being friends. It gets really lonely out here. All on your own."

I smiled and she held my gaze, but I quickly turned away and folded the plans up again.

"So, what's this thing?" she said, picking up the Ask Me a Question magic ball.

"It's just some silly game. You think of a word, and it reckons it can read your mind."

Kitty fiddled with the switch, and the ball burst into life, flashing and playing a little tinkly tune. She held it up to her lips.

"WHERE . . . IS . . . CHARLOTTE'S . . . TREASURE?" she said into the little speaker.

I snorted. "No, it doesn't work like that! You think of something in your head and then answer its questions. It's stupid, really."

Kitty stared at the little device in her hand, closed her eyes, and scrunched up her face. She was obviously taking it very seriously. Then she pressed START and began to answer the questions. When she got to the end the ball went into overdrive mode as it guessed the correct answer. She looked at me, wide-eyed.

"That is *amazing*," she said, staring at the ball for a bit before putting it down on the table. "Right. Come on then, let's go and check out the ice house."

My face dropped. It was going to be very, very dark in there. I couldn't go.

"You go ahead, Kitty. I wouldn't want to . . . you know, take over or anything."

She stopped by the back door. "What? Of course you've got to come. You're the super-riddle-busting champion of the world!"

Her eyes were pleading with me and I couldn't find the words to say no.

"Okay. Well. Perhaps I'll just walk there with you. Hang on a minute."

I went to the front door and got my coat and put on my sneakers. Kitty was waiting for me in the kitchen, and I quickly grabbed the flashlight from the counter. I then realized the Ask Me a Question magic ball was still flashing and beeping loudly on the table. I glanced at the little screen as I went to turn it off. It was scrolling past really quickly. I looked at Kitty, but she had her back to me. I read the little words.

I've guessed it!!!

You are the loser!!!!

Your secret word was . . .

. . . wait for it . . .

BOYFRIEND!!!!!!!!

*Oh boy*, I thought.

# CHAPTER 18
# THE ICE HOUSE

We walked through the wood.

I felt a bit weird after seeing the "boyfriend" thing on the magic ball, but I decided to just ignore it. It probably didn't have anything to do with me; she'd just been trying it out.

"So, where exactly is your house?" I asked. I didn't want to go there, but it would be nice to get a glimpse of it, at least.

"It's over there," she said, waving her hand vaguely. "We can't go near it though. You wouldn't want to be seen by anyone, would you?"

I was about to protest that my parents and I were totally allowed to be at the cottage and weren't hiding, then closed my mouth. I was worried if I said too much she'd start asking questions.

We came out of the forest, and the frozen ground was so hard it hurt the soles of my feet through my thin sneakers.

"It must be amazing having all this space around you," I said as we puffed along. "You can walk the length of our back garden in ten steps."

I wondered if I'd ever see our old house or garden again. It hadn't really felt like home since Gary had moved in. I guessed I wouldn't miss it too much. I thought of Mum and Gary there together. Without me. I pushed the image out of my mind.

Kitty stayed silent and I stopped to take a look behind us. There were the dark woods, and then to the left of that I could just make out the top of a roof.

"Is that the house?" I asked, stretching my neck to try to see more. But Kitty was hurrying in the other direction.

"Look! There's the ice house."

Cut into the side of a hill was a small oval hole containing an iron door, and as we got closer I could see the blackness behind the bars. I shuddered.

"It looks like a dungeon," I said. "That is so creepy."

Kitty crouched down and peered inside. "There's a bit of a drop as you go in and then there's a brick room."

I looked at the outside. It really was a brilliant design. Being built into a small hill meant the whole of the ice house was underground, where it would be coolest.

"Go on then," Kitty said to me. "Open it."

I rattled the iron door, then pulled it gently toward me. It opened easily.

We stood there for a moment, staring into the dark, gaping hole. I could hear a steady *drip, drip, drip* coming from inside, and there was a strong stench of damp. Kitty leaned in.

"Hellllooooooooooo!!!!!" she called, and her voice echoed over and over, tumbling into the darkness. I swallowed as she stared at me, her eyes wide.

"It looks horrible. I can't imagine James and Charlotte playing in there, can you?" I said. "Maybe I was wrong about the ice house?

Maybe there's another kind of frozen place. Somewhere in the kitchen in your house?"

Kitty scowled at me. "Of course it's in here. What else could a frozen place be with the letters *I* and *H*? And remember, it probably looked better when they were little. They lit it up with lanterns and all that."

As I looked into the darkness it made me think of Gary, and my heart began to race like it does after I've been playing soccer.

"I thought this might help," I said, taking my blue flashlight out of my coat pocket. Kitty grinned as if I'd found the treasure already.

"You are a star! Why didn't I think of bringing a flashlight? That is brilliant."

I flicked the switch, then pressed my way through the flashing modes until I got to the steady ON setting.

"It's not exactly the best flashlight in the world, is it?" she said as I shined the feeble light into the darkness.

"Sorry," I said.

There was a reason the flashlight was so dim. Mum had bought it for me after Gary had smashed my light jar, and she said I could put it on when I was in bed if I got really scared. Because the bulb was blue, it didn't shine brightly, so Gary wouldn't spot it under the door. I felt another pang of needing my mum. Badly. I really didn't want to be here, facing a hole of darkness. I was going to have to admit to Kitty that there was no way I was going to go in.

"Okay, who's going first?" she said, kneeling beside the door.

"I—I . . . I'm not sure . . . that I can . . ." I said. The entrance was like a large, gaping mouth ready to swallow me up. It made me think of Gary. And of what he did . . . to our house. I began to shake, hoping that Kitty just thought it was from the cold.

"Fine. I'll go," said Kitty, letting out an almighty huff while simultaneously rolling her eyes. She ducked beneath the low doorway, and I heard her drop down into the chamber.

"Hold on—you haven't got the flashlight!" I said, my voice echoing as I edged closer. I couldn't believe she was so brave she'd just jump into the darkness like that. I waved the flashlight around the best I could.

"It's horrible," Kitty said, her voice really quiet. "I can't see a thing, it's so dark and slippery." Her voice kept fading as she walked around. "It's quite big, I think. I can't see much at the moment. I've got to let my eyes adjust to the dark."

The blue flashlight darted this way and that, but it wasn't bright enough to light anything up.

I listened to her feet scuffing along the brick floor, and then it went quiet.

"Kitty? Are you okay?"

I leaned in a little bit, but I couldn't see a thing.

"Kitty!"

"I'm fine! Point the flashlight over here! There's another chamber toward the back. I'm going to see if there's anything through there."

There was a light blue glow where Kitty was standing, but the flashlight began to flicker. I slapped it against my palm.

"Come back now, Kitty! The batteries are dying!"

I heard some shuffling, and then it went quiet. Water dripped like the ticking of a clock as I listened to the silence.

"Kitty, are you okay?"

"Nate!"

She sounded so far away.

"Kitty? Where are you?"

I banged the flashlight again, and it spluttered into life, then quickly faded. I turned it off and on, but it was dead.

"Kitty, the flashlight isn't working. You've got to try to find a way out!"

"Nate, help me!"

I ducked down, ready to drop through the gap and into the ice house, but then I stopped. It was so dark. So terrifyingly dark. I couldn't do it.

"Kitty? I can't. I can't come in. Just follow my voice, okay? Can you hear me? Kitty!"

"Nate! I'm in the other chamber, and I can't find the door. You've got to help me!"

My heart was pounding. I was faced with a sheet of blackness, and I just couldn't go in.

"Please, Nate, I can't see a thing," said Kitty. I could hear her desperately scrabbling around.

"I—I . . . I can't," I said quietly. I stood up, shivering in the freezing cold.

I ran back to the cottage, not stopping even when I skidded and stumbled to the ground. I couldn't go in there. I just couldn't. And if Kitty wanted to go poking around in some scary ice house, then that was her choice. Surely someone in her home would realize she was missing. Maybe I should go tell them? But I didn't want to be seen. When I got to the cottage Sam was standing in the middle of the living room.

"You're doing the best thing by staying here, you know, Nate," he said. "All of this 'knight in shining armor stuff' just isn't you. No, it's far better to be here. In the warmth. In the light."

I paced up and down beside him. "You're right. She's nothing to do with me. I've got my own problems!"

My head was fuzzy. I sat down on the sofa, and Sam sat down next to me. "Why don't you get the fire going? I mean, it's not like you're going to go and help her."

It didn't feel nice when he said that.

"I mean, so what if she's alone and trapped in the dark? What's it to you?"

I froze for a moment. "But no one knows she's there. I can't go to the house. What if she can't find her way out?"

Sam shrugged his shoulders. "Well, then you're the only one who can help her, aren't you?"

I looked at Sam and he winked. He'd been trying to get me to do something—and it had worked.

"Under the sink!" I shouted. "I bet there're some batteries there. That's where Mum used to keep them at home."

I jumped up and Sam clapped his hands together. "That's a brilliant idea!"

The cupboard under the sink stank of moldy, damp rags. There was a plastic tub full of old scrub brushes and a bag of clothespins and that was it.

"Okay, so that's no good. Now what?" said Sam. He was bouncing around the kitchen like a boxer warming up in the ring. "Come on! You can do this!" He threw a few punches at a shadow on the wall.

"Can you just keep still? I'm trying to think."

I tried to remember if I'd come across anything when I was looking around the cottage for clues to the treasure hunt.

"The alarm clock!" I shouted.

I sprinted upstairs and into my mum's room and grabbed the small white alarm clock on her bedside cabinet. I flicked the back open, and two batteries fell out onto the bed. I quickly unscrewed the bottom of the flashlight and tipped the batteries into my hand, but they were smaller. The ones in Mum's alarm clock were too big to fit. I sat there for a moment, thinking. And then I ran back downstairs.

"Sam, you've got to help me! Do you have *any* ideas?"

"You're asking me a question?" he said.

I stared at him. "What? Yes. Yes, I'm asking you a question. Can you help me? *Please.*"

"Well, I can't believe you're *asking me a question*," he said, emphasizing the words. He was behaving really oddly, and then I realized he was giving me a clue.

I turned away and spotted the Ask Me a Question magic ball on the table.

"Of course!" I said, and I grabbed it and ran to the kitchen. I found a small blunt knife in the drawer and used it to undo the tiny screws. I took the back off the ball and carefully eased out the two batteries, then put them in the flashlight. I twisted the cap back on—and nothing.

"Try them the other way around," said Sam, appearing beside me. I did what he said, quickly screwing the end back on, and then pressed the rubber button. The flashlight gave off a blue glow, and this time it was a little brighter. I was ready.

I ran to the kitchen door and stopped. Sam's yellow color brought warmth to my face.

"You can do this, you know," he said. I smiled at him, then stepped out into the freezing air.

# CHAPTER 19

# INSIDE THE ICE HOUSE

My feet were so cold and wet I couldn't feel them at all by the time I got back to the ice house. I wondered if I was in danger of getting frostbite; maybe I'd end up losing a toe or two. But if I was this cold, how did Kitty feel?

The entrance gate was still open, and there was no sign of Kitty.

"Kitty? Kitty, I'm back, are you all right?" I said, and I waved the dim flashlight into the darkness. I could hear some sniffling noises and some shuffling.

"Nate! You came back!"

I thought she was going to be really angry with me for running off, but she just sounded relieved. I pointed the flashlight in the direction of her voice.

"Just look to where the flashlight is shining and head toward it, okay? Can you see it?"

I moved the light slowly to the left and right, and I heard her moving around in the darkness.

"I can't . . . I can't . . . I'm so cold . . ."

I waved the flashlight again.

"Listen to me, Kitty. You've got to just follow the flashlight. Okay? Can you see it?"

I listened but all I could hear was Kitty quietly crying. My heart was racing. I was going to have to go in.

I took a deep breath, as if I were about to go underwater, ducked down, and scrambled into the ice house and into the blackness. I stood still for a moment, trying not to panic. It was so dark. The blue flashlight barely helped at all. It felt like my face was being covered by a suffocating blanket. I took a few breaths and waited for my eyes to adjust, but not a lot happened. Some water dripped off the ceiling and landed on my cheek, and I jumped.

"Okay, I'm in . . . I'm in the ice house, Kitty, but you've got to h-help . . . You've got to talk so that I can find you . . ." I knew my voice was shaking, but I wanted her to think I was brave.

"I'm here, Nate. I'm here. Just find me, please find me," she said. Her voice was coming from the left, but she sounded distant.

I swallowed. I kept thinking about my mum. And Gary. And the darkness.

"K-Keep talking to me, Kitty, and when you see my flashlight give me a nice big cheer, okay? Keep talking. Tell me something . . . Tell me something about when you were younger . . ."

I trod as carefully as I could, pointing the flashlight down now and then to check my footing.

"I—I remember . . . There was a big dollhouse in the house . . . A big one . . . You c-could . . . You could take the roof off and the front . . ."

I began to walk toward her voice. "That's it. Tell me about the dollhouse. Did you play with it a lot?"

Her voice was helping me keep calm, and I concentrated on what she was saying as I edged deeper into the darkness.

"No. It was Charlotte's dollhouse. She used to play with it. It was her favorite thing. She used to lay in bed at night . . . and stare at the house and imagine she was really tiny, and . . . she could go around all of the rooms . . ."

Her voice was shaking.

"That's great. Keep talking, Kitty. Did your dad tell you that? About Charlotte and her dollhouse?"

I felt my way along a wet, slimy wall. "Oh! I see you! I'm here, Nate! On your left!"

The cold wall came to an end. It was an opening into another room. I pointed the flashlight in the direction of her voice, but I still couldn't see her.

"Okay, can you walk toward the flashlight? Can you edge your way out?"

"I think so . . . I'll go slowly."

I heard her feet shuffling along the floor.

There was a clatter as her foot kicked something, and I heard her stop and scrape the floor with her foot. The flashlight began to flicker.

"Kitty, I don't want to panic you, but you've *got* to hurry up. We need to get out of here. NOW!"

"Hold on, I've found something. I think it's the next clue."

I couldn't believe she was still thinking about that at a time like this. "Are you serious?! Come on! If you don't come now, I'm getting out of here right this second!" My voice echoed around the room.

"I'm coming! Don't leave me."

Her pale face suddenly appeared in the beam from my flashlight and I gasped. She smiled. She looked so pleased to see me.

"Thank you! Thank you, Nate."

"Come on. Let's get out of here," I said, and as I turned, the flashlight died.

Someone was screaming. At first I thought it was Kitty, but it didn't sound quite like her.

"Stop it. It's fine, I can see the doorway!"

The screaming carried on. I put my hands over my ears to block it out.

"Calm down! We're nearly there now. That's enough! I said ENOUGH!"

The screaming stopped and was replaced with shuddering sobs.

"The door is just over there, we can make it. Okay? Let's just go slowly and steadily."

I saw a dim semicircle of light in the distance that grew brighter and brighter as I headed toward it. Before I knew it, I was scrambling through the hole and squinting in the daylight. Kitty stood in front of me.

"Nate. What's going on? Are you okay? Why were you screaming like that? You frightened me."

I stared back at her, blinking. It had been *me*? *I* had been the one screaming?

"I—I . . . I'm okay. I've got to go. I've got to go back now."

She looked at me with her head to one side. "You didn't sound okay."

Kitty was holding something in her hand. It was a gray tin. She held it up and smiled.

"I've found it, Nate. I kicked it with my foot. The next riddle is going to be in here, I just know it."

She began to open the tin, but I didn't care any more. I just needed to get to the cottage. "I'm sorry. I've got to go."

I turned away and I ran. I ran to the cottage, and I didn't look back.

# CHAPTER 20
# AFRAID OF THE DARK

I put my wet sneakers beside the roaring fire and sat watching the flames as I hugged my knees. Sam was sitting on the sofa but hadn't said anything. Every now and then he looked at me as if he were waiting for me to start. Waiting for me to say something. He folded his arms.

"So, are you going to tell me then? Why you're so afraid of the dark?" he said.

I breathed slowly onto my knees but didn't say anything.

His face had scrunched into a scowl. "Okay, you don't want to talk. I get it. But what I want to know is how could your mum just let him come into *her* house and boss her around like that? What was *wrong* with her?"

"I know . . . I know how it sounds. It sounds like Mum let him walk all over her, but it wasn't like that at all. Gary *controlled* things without you even realizing he was doing it. I never once heard him shout. He never tried to hurt us or anything. It was as if it was all going on like a rage in his head. Sometimes . . . Sometimes you could see it behind his eyes."

The room was silent apart from the crackling of the fire. "And the dark?"

I sighed. "Like I said, Gary was clever. We didn't really notice what he was doing to start with."

Sam leaned forward and rested his chin on his hand as he listened. And then I told him. I told him why I was so terrified of the dark.

"We were all sitting at the dinner table one evening when the light bulb above us went *pop*. Mum put her knife and fork down to go and get a new one from under the sink, but Gary put his hand on her arm.

"'Leave it, Fiona,' he said. 'I'll do it after dinner.'

"I leaned back on my chair to look out the window. It was getting dark, but the hallway light was on and we could still see what we were eating. Gary chatted about a computer problem he was trying to sort out at work, and then Mum tried to join in and told him about our old laptop that had stopped working because it had a disease. I didn't know why she said it; it was the stupidest thing she'd ever said.

"'Virus, Mum. It's called a virus,' I said, hoping that Gary would stop laughing in that strange way of his.

"'You're such a silly-billy, aren't you, Fiona? That's what I love about you,' he said, as he patted her arm.

"Gary didn't replace the bulb after dinner, so Mum changed it herself after he'd gone to bed. The next morning when I came down for breakfast, Mum and Gary were in the kitchen talking.

"'But I don't understand it,' she said. 'I changed the bulb last night. Has it definitely blown again? We've never had any problems with that light before.'

"I hovered in the kitchen while Mum searched under the sink for another bulb.

"'Don't touch it now, Fiona. It might not be safe. I'll take a look at the fitting later and see why it keeps going.'

"Mum picked up her cell phone and began to text someone. 'I'll see if Laura's husband can pop over and take a look. He's an electrician. He won't mind.'

"Gary walked up to her and calmly took her cell phone out of her hand and slid it into his back pocket.

"'There's no need for that. We don't need this Laura's husband bothering us, do we? You've got me here now.'

"He kissed Mum's forehead and tapped me on the head as he went into the living room.

"As far as I know, that was the last time she saw her cell phone. She told me she'd accidentally dropped it and was going to get another, but she never seemed to get around to it. I suspect he never gave it back to her. We didn't have a light in the dining room for a few weeks, and then he said the living room bulb had gone."

My throat caught.

"He said . . . He said that another bulb had blown and until he'd looked at the wiring we shouldn't switch any of the lights on."

Sam gasped. "What, ever? In the whole house?"

I nodded.

"He'd been living with us for a nearly a year then. Like I said, it all happened slowly."

I suddenly felt an overwhelming urge to cry, and I took a deep breath to stop myself.

"Mum . . . Mum was just shocked, I think. I don't know what he was like with her when I wasn't around, but I can imagine it . . . it wasn't good. When I got home from school Mum would keep the kitchen light on and shut the door and I'd sit in there and do my homework and we'd chat and she'd cook dinner while Gary was at work, but as soon as we heard his car pull onto the driveway she'd quickly switch the light off. One evening he came straight into the kitchen still wearing his shoes and coat. Mum had turned the light off when she'd heard his car, so we were sitting in the dark as usual, but he was acting all weird, pacing around the kitchen like he was really angry. He dragged a kitchen chair to the middle of the room, then stood on it and felt the light bulb, flinching when it scorched his hand. It was hot from where we'd had it on. Mum started to apologize, saying I needed the light so I could do my homework, but he didn't say anything. He walked out of the kitchen and went to their bedroom, where he stayed for the rest of the evening."

My hands were trembling while I talked, and I stuffed them under my legs to keep them still.

"The next day he removed every light bulb in the house."

"He did what?!"

I just looked at Sam, and he shook his head and stared at the floor.

"If that had happened to me, I'd be freaked out by the dark too."

I gave him a weak smile. "We lived like that for months. The summer wasn't too bad, as it was light in the evenings and the mornings, but winter was awful."

"What if someone came to visit? Didn't they notice something wrong?" said Sam.

I shook my head. "No one came around. By the time Gary removed the light bulbs we hadn't had any visitors for weeks. Mum had stopped inviting people because Gary would make the air all tense. I remember her friend Laura turning up one evening with a bottle of wine and some flowers. I think she was worried about Mum, to be honest. I was listening upstairs, and Mum turned her away, saying now wasn't a good time, but all they were doing was watching television. I think she was just doing whatever made life easier, and that meant not letting on that Gary was the way he was."

The wind was picking up outside and whistling over the top of the chimney like it was blowing across a bottle.

"You know what, Nate? You were so brave to go into that ice house. To confront your fears like that."

I shrugged. I hadn't felt brave; I'd felt terrified.

The two of us sat in silence for a bit.

"Where do you think your mum is, Nate?" said Sam.

I swallowed, not looking at him. The thing that had been worrying me for so long pushed itself to the front of my brain. A horrible thought trying to be let in, to be made real.

"I think she's gone back," I said. "I think she's gone back to Gary."

When I next looked up, Sam had vanished.

# CHAPTER 21
# OFF TO THE POTTING SHED

The more I thought about it, the more it made sense. Gary always did have some kind of weird control over Mum. She must have given in to him, yet again. She'd probably called him from a pay phone when she went shopping and he'd managed to convince her to go back. She just couldn't live without him. Or worse, maybe, just maybe, this had been her plan all along—to get me out of the house so that she could go back and live with him on her own, happily ever after. Maybe *I* was the issue. Perhaps if *I* wasn't around, then Gary would be easier to live with. That's why she brought me here. She couldn't exactly take me to Grandma's with them not talking to each other any more. Where else was she going to take me? I paced around the front room. Was that it? Had I been left here? All alone in an abandoned cottage? My heart was racing and I felt dizzy. As I walked from one side of the room to the other, Sam appeared in the armchair. I was pleased he was here.

"You don't know what's happened," he said.

I rubbed at my forehead. "I know I don't, but . . . I can't think straight . . ."

Sam watched me walking up and down. "Well, let's look at the facts. Was your mum unhappy before you left?"

I perched on the edge of the sofa, squeezing my hands together. I thought about how anxious Mum had been. She used to frown all the time, and she had a permanent pool of tears in the bottoms of her eyes. "Yes. She was really miserable."

Sam nodded. "Right. So she was unhappy enough to pack her bags, find a car, and whisk you away in the middle of the night . . . How was she when you got here? Did she seem miserable then? Did she act like she'd made some big mistake?"

I stood up again. I couldn't keep still.

I remembered when we'd arrived she'd got upset about the chicken being outside on the window ledge, but the next day she'd seemed fine. In fact, when we'd been hitting the rug with the sticks in the garden, I think that was the first time I'd see her laugh for *years*.

"No . . . I . . . er . . . I think she was happy."

"Okay," said Sam. "Let's think about it again. Nate, do you think your mum has gone back to live with Gary? That she deliberately brought you here so that she could go back and live happily ever after with him? Do you really think that?"

I looked at Sam and I sighed.

"I don't know, Sam," I said. "I really don't know."

Sam gazed at me sadly from the armchair, and then he faded away again into a yellow haze. I opened the wood stove's door and was raking the ash when I heard something in the kitchen.

"Hello? It's me! I brought you a cheese scone. To make up for the ice house thing. I'm sorry you were so scared."

Kitty was standing by the door clutching another brown paper bag in her hands.

"I didn't hear you come in. Don't you ever knock?"

She shrugged. "Sorry."

She rustled the brown paper bag toward me.

"I warmed it up in the oven and it's still hot. I wasn't sure if you were still going to be here."

I kept silent as she walked in and passed me the bag. The smell of warm cheese filled my nostrils and my mouth watered. Her eyes darted around the room, and I was sure she was looking for signs that I was really here all on my own. She caught me watching her and quickly clapped her hands together.

"Well, eat the scone then! And I'll tell you all about the next clue."

I reached into the bag and took out a warm scone. I took a small bite. It tasted of butter, with a little salt, and strong, creamy cheddar. It was possibly the best scone I could have ever imagined eating. It was even better than her butterscotch muffin.

I sat down at the dining table, and she pulled a gray tin out of her satchel. It was the one she had been holding in her hand when we'd gotten out of the ice house. Opening it up, she took out a card that had the same handwriting as the other clues. She held it up so that I could read and eat at the same time:

CLUE 3

A HUNTSMAN BRIGHT AM I,

Kitty smiled. "It's going to be an easy one—'you'll find me boxed in green.' All we need to do is find a green box."

She looked around the room and at all the ornaments on the mantelpiece.

"It's no use looking here. I've already searched everywhere," I said, pushing the last of the crumbs into my mouth. "There's definitely no green box in this cottage."

Kitty frowned as she walked around the living room.

"Okay. And I guess it would be a bit odd to hide the next clue in the same area as the last," she said. "And it's almost too simple. A green box . . . There must be more to it than that. What about the huntsman? Up on high?"

Kitty frowned, and then her face lit up.

"Maybe the green box has something to do with gardening. The shed! There's an old potting shed near the house. We could start there."

She headed to the back door.

"Are you coming? We're getting closer to finding Charlotte's treasure now. William only ever left three clues—the treasure must be in this green box."

I looked down at my empty plate. I was still thinking about what I'd said to Sam and if Mum had actually left me. The thought clutched at my heart, and I felt it tighten its grip.

Kitty was watching me. Waiting.

"Okay," I said. "Let's go and take a look."

———————————

We walked through the woods, but when we got to the edge, Kitty stopped. It was almost as if she didn't know the way.

"You said it was near the house, didn't you? The potting shed?" I asked.

"It's this way," she said, and she turned right and began walking down a hill in the opposite direction. It looked like we were skirting around the bottom of the garden.

"Wouldn't it have been quicker to have gone the other way when we came out of the woods? Past the maze?" I asked. "Aren't we just going in a big circle?"

"No," said Kitty firmly. "This is the way."

She was lying. I just knew it. I'd seen the map, and she was walking in the opposite direction to where we needed to go. It was as if she was deliberately trying to avoid her house, but why? What was she hiding? I could see the edge of the house out the corner of my eye and was going to stop and have a proper look when Kitty ducked behind a high hedge.

"Nate! You might get spotted."

I brushed against the shrubbery and a dusting of snow fell on my head. We were right at the bottom of the garden. When we got to the end of a long green hedge, Kitty carried straight on. We were heading farther away from the house. I was confused.

"Shouldn't we have turned left?" I asked, struggling to keep up with her.

"No, this is the best route," she said. "It's not far."

Kitty darted between various shrubs and overgrown arches in the garden, and I kept behind her, running as quickly as I could. We passed a rectangular pond that was full of frozen brown sludge and what looked like a stone seat that had cracked in two. I tried to get a look at the house, but there were overgrown shrubs blocking the view.

"Keep up! Come on!" said Kitty, and then she turned left, back up toward the house.

She'd deliberately skirted around the bottom of the garden, taking me in a big semicircle, keeping the house out of sight. I only managed to glimpse the corner of a wall before we got to the potting shed. I pulled open the little wooden door, and we stepped inside into the gloom.

Hanging on hooks around the shed was an assortment of garden tools. A workbench ran along one side beneath a window so dirty you couldn't see out. There were lots of black plastic pots on the bench and a small mound of earth with a trowel sticking out of it. Up on a shelf was a big mug with *Head Gardener* written on the front. It felt like William Blakelore was going to walk in and carry on potting his seeds at any moment. Kitty began to whisper.

"I'll start over here. You take a look through that old cabinet."

She put her brown satchel down, climbed up on to the bench, and inspected the tools.

"Remember, it's a green box we're after. It must be in here somewhere."

I went over to the old metal filing cabinet. It had three drawers, and when I pulled on the top one it opened with a screech. Inside was a bundle of scrunched-up plastic bags, which I took out.

"Urgh, there's something dead in here," I said, looking at a curled-up, furry skeleton in the corner. "It's a mouse. It must have gotten stuck, poor thing."

I stared at the little mouse for a moment, then covered it again with the plastic bags and closed the drawer.

Kitty was clattering around, stopping now and then to hold something up to the light, probably checking whether it was green or not. The next two drawers were full of old gardening books and magazines.

"This is such good fun, isn't it, Nate? I'm so pleased you're here with me."

She stopped what she was doing and gave me a goofy smile, but I didn't smile back. I was freezing. The shed was dark and it stank and I really didn't want to be here.

"I mean, we're good friends now, aren't we? We're a proper team!"

She giggled but I didn't laugh. Being dragged around wasn't my idea of fun. It was okay for her; she had her nice warm mansion with its heating, cozy fire, and parents waiting for her. This was all just a game, and I was just going along with her like a stupid plaything. And I had far more important things to be worrying about.

"Actually, Kitty, I don't think we're going to find anything here," I said, ignoring what she'd said. "Maybe we should give up."

She climbed down from the bench, dropped to her knees, and crawled under it, emerging with a pair of old brown boots that she tipped upside down and shook. A shower of dirt fell out onto the floor.

"Give up? But he *must* have hidden it here," she said. "We're so close to the end, we can't give up now." She was beginning to sound desperate again.

"Well, you can carry on looking, if you like. I've had enough. I'm going back," I said.

"But we only just got here," said Kitty. "I thought we were friends? Aren't we?" Her big blue eyes sparkled in the cold air.

"I, well, I guess . . . But I've got to go. Sorry, Kitty."

Kitty stood up and glared at me with her hands on her hips.

"What time are your parents going to be back again?" she asked. "Shouldn't you have left them a note saying where you were going?"

I got ready to say something about them not being worried but shut my mouth. She was obviously working out that my story wasn't adding up. How long would it be before she told someone?

"Look, Kitty. I'm sure you'll manage to solve the clues all on your own. But count me out."

Her jaw dropped as I made my way to the door.

"I'm going back to the cottage now. And just so you don't waste more time coming around again, I think it's best that you carry on with the treasure hunt on your own. Okay?"

I walked out into the bitterly cold air and left her standing there, openmouthed. My footprints were still visible in the light snow, but rather than follow their line I headed across the lawn. It would be much quicker going the other way, and I could just dart between the shrubs to keep out of view of anyone.

I felt guilty for talking to her like that, but her treasure hunt really was not my problem. I couldn't understand why she was so desperate to solve it. It was just a stupid thing created for some bored kids many years ago.

I walked past a large concrete fountain that had icicles hanging from it and I started to speed up. I was out in the open now, so I glanced to the right and got my first proper look at Kitty's house.

I stopped.

Across the snowy lawn was the mansion I'd pictured so many times in my head. In my mind I'd seen a large, grand building with lots of white-edged windows of all different sizes. Some of the windows would have stretched from the ground to the ceiling, and some would be arched with maybe a semicircle of colored glass fanning across the top. There would be a wide, glazed door that would open onto a patio area surrounded by tall marble statues of Greek gods. All those rooms would have needed roaring fireplaces back when it was built, so standing to attention across the roof would be an orderly line of chimneys. Yes, in my mind it was a magnificent, stately home.

But it wasn't like that at all. There were lots of windows, but most of them had gray boards blocking them up. Clambering up the side of the house was a mass of ivy that was strangling a crumbling chimney stack. Across the roof were giant, gaping holes as if a huge monster had bitten great chunks out of it. Blue plastic sheeting covered one section of the roof, probably put there as an attempt to cover another hole. It flapped loose in the wind like a blinking eye.

The patio area did have statues as I'd imagined, but they looked like zombies, covered in thick green moss and black slime. One was even missing its head.

I was stunned.

Kitty appeared beside me.

"B-But I don't understand," I said. "I thought . . . I thought your dad owned a big company and . . ."

I looked at her face, and she seemed to be close to crying.

"It's not how it looks," she said. "I'm not . . . I've not been lying." She looked worried, scared even.

This was why she'd been trying to steer me away from the house. So that I didn't see what an utter ruin it was.

"But . . . how can you live here? I mean, are you even allowed to?"

Kitty pressed her lips together but didn't say anything. I looked her straight in the eye.

"Kitty?"

She kept opening her mouth to say something but then closing it again as if she'd thought better of it.

"I thought if you lived in a mansion, you'd have a lot of money," I said. "Did your dad lose it all? Did the business fail?"

Kitty nodded slowly. She bit on her lip and I waited for her to say more, but she kept silent.

"And is it safe? Is it safe to live there?" I said. Suddenly William's drafty old cottage didn't seem so bad after all.

"We . . . We can only use a couple of rooms," she said.

It looked like a skeleton of a house. It certainly wasn't a home.

"Why did you lie to me, Kitty? You could have told me the truth."

Kitty huffed. "I didn't lie, exactly. It was *you* that assumed I was some spoiled little rich kid with heaps of money. I said nothing of the sort."

She pulled her woolly hat down farther.

"Anyway, if we're not careful someone is going to spot you and realize *you're* staying in a cottage that doesn't belong to you. We've got to get moving."

She buried her fists into her coat pockets and ran behind the tall, hedged maze. I took a final look at the house and followed her.

Kitty stopped at the entrance to the maze. Her words had panicked me a bit. Were we actually allowed to stay in the cottage? Mum had taken us there, but did she have permission? Maybe we shouldn't have gone there at all. And how close was Kitty to telling her dad or someone else?

"Nate, are your parents in trouble with the police? Is that why you're hiding out? Are your mum and dad criminals?" Kitty looked worried.

"No. It's nothing like that. I know how it looks, but you're wrong. Okay?"

"I don't believe you," she said, folding her arms.

I stood next to her and casually brushed some snow off a little wooden sign that was next to the maze entrance. "It's complicated. I made the mistake of assuming things about you. Please don't do the same about me."

She looked at me for a bit.

"I'll think about it," she said. And she began to walk away.

I took a long breath. It was over. She was going to go home and tell her parents about me, and then the police would come, and then someone from social services when they saw I was on my own, and then who knew where I'd end up?

I looked up at the tall green maze beside me and thought of poor Charlotte, running in there on a freezing New Year's Eve and not coming out again. I shivered. I glanced down at the brown sign and traced the words with my finger.

# THE TURNER-WRIGHT GARDEN MAZE

## A LABYRINTH OF BOX HEDGING

### (SCIENTIFIC NAME: *BUXUS SEMPERVIRENS*)

Box. This type of hedge was called a box.

"Kitty! Wait up!" I yelled, just as she reached the edge of the woods. "Come back! I think I've solved the clue!"

# CHAPTER 22

# TELLING KITTY ABOUT DAD

Kitty turned around.

"I've found it!" I yelled. "I've found the green box!"

She didn't move, so I pointed my finger toward the sign.

"You've got to come and see this!"

She began to walk toward me and then her walk turned into a run. She joined me, panting, searching around on the floor. "Where? Where is it?"

I grinned and held my hand up to the maze. "This is your green box."

I showed her the sign, and she read it out loud.

"A labyrinth of box. Genius! He was a genius. A green 'box'! Of course! I'd never have thought of that," she said. We both peered in through the overgrown entrance.

"Have you ever been to the middle of the maze before?" I asked.

Kitty shook her head. She looked pale, and her lips had turned blue again. She stared at me and blinked a few times, and I could almost see her brain whirling. It was getting dark. In another half an hour it would be so dark we wouldn't be able to see where we were going.

More darkness meant another day had passed without any

sign of Mum. Maybe she was sitting at home right now. With Gary. Watching TV. My stomach knotted.

"We need to come back in the morning, Kitty. We can't risk going in there now."

"But Charlotte's treasure is in there, I know it! Let's just give it a try and see, shall we? We can always turn back if it looks too complicated."

Kitty was jiggling around on the spot. I shook my head, and she rolled her eyes.

"Okay, okay, you win. We'll come back first thing tomorrow. And then maybe we'll finally solve the whole thing. Oh, Nate, it's so wonderful to have you here to help me. I could never have solved all these riddles on my own."

I gave her a weak smile. She wanted to find the treasure in Charlotte's memory, I got that, and I was pleased I'd been able to help. But she was so obsessed with it, it was also kind of weird.

We slowly headed back to the woods. Kitty could have turned off toward the house, but she stayed by my side.

"You must really love your family. To do this for your aunt Charlotte and your dad," I said.

"Why, don't you love yours?"

I was going to tell her what a great family I had, but I'd had enough of lying.

"My dad moved out when I was six," I began.

"Moved out? But isn't your dad here? Renovating the cottage with your mum?"

I sighed. I'd sort of forgotten that bit. Kitty looked puzzled but not angry.

"No, he's not here," I said. "He left us years ago."

And as we walked, I told her why.

---

Carrie was the reason Dad moved out. If she hadn't come along he'd still be living with us now, Gary would never have moved into our house and our lives, and I wouldn't be staying in a freezing cold, abandoned cottage all on my own.

Carrie lived in New York, but she worked for the same company as Dad and would come for meetings at the London office. That's how they met. That's how she stole him from us.

He told me all about her after we'd gotten home from my school sports day. My team hadn't won the cup, but I had a heavy gold medal around my neck that I'd been given for being the day's "Most Enthusiastic Supporter," which basically meant I'd cheered my friends on and hadn't booed the other kids.

Mum hadn't come to watch that day. She'd said she had an appointment to get her hair cut, which should have warned me that something was up. It was odd for her to arrange to go to the hairdresser on my sports day. I didn't complain too much though, as Dad was coming, which was a proper treat. He'd cheered and waved at me from the sideline and laughed and joked with the other parents. I didn't have a clue about the bombshell he was about to drop.

When we got home Mum was still out, and I'd dived onto the sofa and studied the medal around my neck.

"You know I love you, don't you, Nate?"

I looked up at Dad's face and I knew then, in that split second, that whatever he was about to say was going to change my life. He was biting his top lip, and his eyes kept darting around the room. He took a deep breath and then began to explain that Carrie, an American, was the love of his life, and that even though he loved Mum, nothing could have prepared him for how he would feel about this new woman.

I didn't say anything.

There had been no arguing, no fighting at home, no signs of anything wrong. I felt a great weight smash me in my stomach, sending me somersaulting out of control into the air.

I waited to hear what he was going to say next, hoping he'd tell me that it was all just some kind of stupid joke, but he didn't.

"I'm getting a transfer from work. I'm moving to New York."

It was then that I spoke up. "But I don't want to live in New York. I want to live here."

Dad did a nervous laugh and ruffled my hair, but I glared at him. This was far from funny. "No, buddy, you misunderstood me."

Buddy? He never called me buddy. He was turning American in front of my eyes.

"No, what I mean is I'm going to live in New York with Carrie. I'm going to be just across the Atlantic. How about that?"

I remember gasping out loud as the full meaning of what he was saying hit me. "What? Without us? Without me?"

He did that stupid, nervous laugh again. "You can come and stay whenever you like. Won't that be amazing? And I'll be back every few months for work. We can spend whole weekends together, and in fact, I've been thinking about this a lot, and do you know, I bet you we'll actually have a much more special time together, as we'll have planned it properly. How about that?"

I wanted to push him. I wanted to press my hands against his chest and push him away. "But what about Mum?"

Dad couldn't look me in the eyes then. "She'll come around. It's all been a bit of a shock, but she knows it's the right thing to do."

I suddenly took a large breath, refilling my shriveled lungs. "The right thing for you, you mean!"

He put a hand on my arm. "Nate, I can't help how I feel. I'm sorry, buddy, but you'll just have to get used to it."

My head was pounding and I could feel tears rush to my eyes. I wouldn't let him see how upset I was, I *wouldn't*, so I ran from the room, pelting upstairs as he yelled after me.

"I'm sorry, Nate. I'm so sorry."

"That's so sad," said Kitty quietly. "I'm sure your dad didn't mean to hurt everyone, but it couldn't have been easy for you."

I nodded. She didn't ask why I'd lied about being in the cottage with both my parents, and I was grateful for that. I'm not sure what I would have said if she had.

It was on the tip of my tongue to tell her what happened next. Dancing around like one of the tiny snowflakes that were beginning to flutter down around us. I could tell her everything, about Mum meeting Gary, about the monster he became, running away, and her going missing. I could then say that I thought she'd gone back to him. That she'd never really stood up to him and he had some weird power over her. I was just thinking how on earth I would start when we reached William's Gate leading into the cottage garden. It was dark now, and I needed to get in and get all the lights on.

"So, I'll see you tomorrow?" Kitty said. "We can solve this thing. Together!"

She gave me a big smile and I nodded. Kitty turned to go, but then came back. Her face looked all serious.

"Thank you, Nate," she said. "Thank you for helping." And then she ran back up the hill toward her crumbling home.

I opened the iron gate, my stomach churning when I thought about tomorrow. There was something I had been pushing out of my mind along with the worry about my mum. I was scared that if I thought about it too much, I'd completely fall to pieces.

But there was no escaping it.

Tomorrow was my twelfth birthday.

# CHAPTER 23

# CHARLIE AND DEXTER

Snow was falling heavily and I could hear my breath and my feet crunching on the frozen ground as I walked across the garden to the cottage. By the back door was the chicken, her eyes half-closed, covered in a light layer of snow. I eased the door open and she stood up, cocked her head from one side to the other, and then jumped over the step and inside. I followed, quickly shutting the door.

The chicken ruffled her feathers and then strutted around the kitchen, pecking at the odd crumb on the floor. She didn't look scared at all. I opened the out-of-date crackers, crumbled a couple up in my hand, and made a little pile down in the corner. The chicken did a funny, fast walk to get to them, then stabbed at them with her beak. I filled a cereal bowl with water and placed that next to the crumbs.

Under the sink was an old washing-up bowl. I took a scarf from a hook by the door and put it in the bottom of the bowl, making a kind of nest.

"There you go. A little bed for you," I said, putting it down next to the chicken. "I'll let you out whenever you want, but for now you can stay here and keep nice and warm."

The chicken happily jabbed at the crackers, and I closed the kitchen door so that she couldn't wander into the rest of the house.

The living room was freezing, and I knelt in front of the wood stove and raked the ash into a flat surface using the poker. The wood basket only had a few small pieces left and a handful of kindling. I also only had a few cubes of firelighters left, but I decided not to worry about that for now, and I layered the small pieces of kindling over the white cubes and lit a match.

"You told her about your dad then?"

I dropped the match into the fire and spun around. Sam was sitting with his legs hanging over the side of the armchair.

"Do you think you could kind of give me a warning when you're about to arrive?" I said, holding my hand to my chest. "You nearly gave me a heart attack."

Sam smirked, his yellow glow warming the corner of the room. I shut the door of the stove, and the flames flickered as they caught the kindling.

"So, your dad went off to America. Then what happened?"

I sat cross-legged by the fire. "After his talk with me, Dad moved to New York within days. Our family didn't exist any more. They never admitted it, but it was obvious that the plans for him to move to New York had been sorted out weeks before."

"Grown-ups do that kind of thing all the time," said Sam.

I nodded. I was always the last to know about anything. Dad leaving, us coming here.

"After he'd gone, Mum walked around the house in a daze. She'd smile when I came into the room, but her face crumpled when she thought I wasn't looking. She got really thin too and stopped doing anything around the house. Grandma and Granddad came by when they could and made sure we had enough food in the cupboards and that my school uniform was clean. I overheard them talking to Mum one evening.

"'You've got to pull yourself together, Fiona. Nate needs his mum. He's lost his dad, so now it's time for you to step up to the mark. Get this family back on track!'

"And after a while, she did.

"She got herself a job working at a real estate agent's, and before long we found ourselves back in a routine. She'd make a packed lunch for her and one for me, and we'd both leave the house at the same time each morning, me to school and her off to work. Every day she'd give me a kiss on the top of my head:

"'Have a good day, darling.'

"I used to huff and act as if I didn't like it when she said that, but inside I was just so pleased to see her happy again. Mum's real smile was starting to come back."

The fire was ready for a bigger log, so I carefully opened the door and placed one on top of the burning kindling. I was getting good at it now.

"And what about your dad? Did you keep in touch?" asked Sam.

I closed the wood stove's door. "He used to call twice a week. He'd promise he'd visit, but then he'd say that he was too busy. They'd bought a new apartment that they were having renovated, so he'd say he was coming, but then he couldn't because their new kitchen was being fitted or they were choosing a sofa or something. As if I cared."

Sam's glow dimmed. "Haven't you seen him since?"

"Yes. He came back about a year later. He looked so different. He had this silly little beard on his chin that looked like it had been stuck on. He took me out for burgers and chips, but I refused to eat anything and told him his beard looked stupid. He pretended not to be hurt, but I could see it had upset him.

"'How's your mum doing?' he asked. 'I hear she's seeing someone else?'

"Mum had met Gary by then. She must have mentioned it to him. Gary designed websites for a living, and she'd been introduced to him through work. I'd noticed she did a lot more singing and a lot more looking in the mirror.

"'She's fine,' I told Dad. 'Gary is great. He does loads with me, and we go out together all the time. To be honest with you, he's like a proper dad.'

"Dad's face fell. I knew I'd hurt him, but I didn't care. From then on, every time I spoke to him on the phone or wrote him an email, I told him how amazing Gary was and how I really didn't miss him at all. But I did. I missed him terribly."

I watched the fire glowing orange as the log began to burn.

"I don't know why I said that to Dad."

I looked up, but Sam was gone.

I put on every light in the cottage, then headed to the kitchen to check on the chicken. The cracker crumbs had all gone, and she was sitting on top of the scarf in her washing-up bowl. She put her head on one side and watched me for a moment, then her head sunk into her neck and she shut her eyes. It felt nice being able to help her out of the cold, even if she was just a chicken.

When I went back into the front room, Sam was standing by the fire. He looked taller. It was like he was waiting to tell me something. I sat on the sofa, pulling my legs up. I felt tingling in the tips of my fingers and toes. Something was about to happen—I could feel it. And then, without saying a word, Sam waved his hand just like he had before and the wall began to evaporate.

"Whoa . . . How . . . How do you do that?" I asked, blinking at the shimmering space that was beginning to form before me. The picture started to come into focus. I could see a crowd of people, and then they blurred and suddenly we were looking at a boy wearing a cream baseball cap with a *B* on the front, a shiny blue shirt, and cream shorts. He had a baseball gripped in his left hand, and he was staring right at me. He gave a subtle nod of his head, then pulled his arm back, and *whoosh* . . . the ball was coming right at me. I ducked to the side and hid my head in the sofa cushion, but nothing happened. When I sat up the image had pulled back to reveal a huge baseball field. It was a hot summer's day and a game was in full swing as Sam began to talk . . .

"Charlie was the *best* pitcher the Boxton Blues had ever had. *EVER.* The rest of the team didn't take baseball that seriously, but Charlie? Well, Charlie was outside every night after school, practicing his pitches over and over and over again. He was *so* dedicated."

My jaw hung open as I watched the kids running around the field, dust flying beneath their feet. Charlie, the pitcher in the middle, threw another ball, and there was a crack as the bat hit the ball and sent it rocketing upward. Everyone stood and stared as it soared up and up and up until it paused, then began to plummet back down toward the ground. Charlie threw his baseball cap on the ground and pelted across the field, diving to the earth and sliding along in the dust to catch the ball in one outstretched hand. The crowd went crazy.

"Awesome," I said, glancing at Sam. He moved his hand and the image blurred and began to change. This time the space was smaller. Charlie was there again, this time in jeans and T-shirt, and he now appeared to be in a back garden. He had another baseball in his hand, and he was staring at a silver tin can that had been placed on top of a fence post. Beside Charlie was another boy dressed in a bright green baseball uniform. He was slapping his hands together and talking in Charlie's ear as if he was encouraging him. There was something I recognized about the boy. He had a green glow, just like the imaginary friend before, Meena, had a purple one and like Sam had a yellow one.

I watched as Charlie eyeballed the can, and then *WHAM!* He threw the ball, and the can somersaulted into the air and fell onto the ground with a clatter. The other boy whooped and clapped his hands together.

"Is that . . . Is that Charlie's imaginary . . . friend?" I asked, pointing to the boy in green.

"Yep. That's Dexter. He's good. *Really* good. His dedication is unbelievable. He spent hours with Charlie, practicing his pitching. But things . . . Things didn't work out so well for Charlie in this case . . ."

They looked so happy. Charlie reset the tin can as Dexter punched the air and cheered him on.

"Why not?" I said. "What happened?"

"Well, Charlie's team won the league that year. He played his best baseball ever. He really was their star player."

I smiled as Charlie threw the ball again and knocked the can flying. Dexter ran around the garden, waving his arms above his head. He had green eyes and a big wide grin. He looked like he'd be really fun to hang out with. But then the image began to blur. I leaned forward on the sofa. Suddenly we were back at the baseball field again, but this time the game was over. Charlie was being held up on his teammates' shoulders as he waved a shiny gold trophy in the air.

"They circled that field seven times. Seven! The crowd went crazy," said Sam.

They all looked so happy I almost wanted to applaud them myself. An older, chubby man was following the group of kids, clapping madly with a big grin on his face.

"That's Coach Benson," said Sam.

I watched as he reached up and patted Charlie on the back. "I'm so proud of you, boy. You've made this team complete, and if it weren't for you, we wouldn't be holding this trophy today."

"Thanks, Coach Benson," said Charlie, before his teammates carried him off on another lap of the field.

The image faded again and now we were in Charlie's bedroom. He was asleep, the trophy under his arm.

"He slept with it under his arm for three nights running. But that was it. Not long after they won the league, Charlie gave up baseball completely."

"What?" I said, confused. "He gave it up? Why?"

As I asked the question Sam's color faded and he moved his arm, and the image changed again. I was back at the baseball field, but this time it looked like they were training.

"Coach Benson brought in a new kid—Elliot."

I could see the coach with Charlie and another, smaller boy. They were talking about something, but Charlie had his arms folded and he didn't look happy.

"Coach Benson told Charlie he wanted him to take Elliot under his wing and teach him all he knew about pitching. He said they needed more than one strong pitcher on their team."

"Charlie tried it for a bit, showed him how to stand, and taught him about curveballs and sliders and all that . . . but, you know . . . it just didn't work out, so he quit."

I watched the image change and saw Charlie throw the ball on the floor and stomp off the field. Following behind him was Dexter, his green glow now a dull dishwater color.

"He quit? Their star player *quit*? Just because they brought in a new player? Why would he do that?"

Sam shrugged. "He took it personally. But it wasn't Coach Benson's fault. They needed a team of good players, not just Charlie. Dexter tried his best to talk him out of it, but it was no use. He joined another team and, well . . . Let's just say things were not the same."

Sam waved his hand again, and this time we were at another baseball field with a team dressed in red. Charlie was sitting on a bench looking incredibly fed up. Behind him was Dexter, his green color almost gone as he watched his friend looking so miserable.

"His new coach, Coach Rudge, wasn't great. He hardly picked Charlie to play at all. So in the end he just stopped playing altogether."

I suddenly felt angry. "But that's so stupid! What about Coach Benson? Couldn't he have just gone back to his old team? He'd have taken him back, right?"

Sam sighed. "Coach Benson saw him at a game one weekend. He noticed he wasn't getting any play, so he came over at the end to talk to him. 'You can come back to us anytime, you know, Charlie. If your new coach isn't working out for you, we'd have you back in a millisecond.'"

"And?" I said. "What did he say?"

"He was tempted, I know that much. But that new kid, Elliot, had been their pitcher all day. Dexter had whispered into Charlie's ear: 'Do it, Charlie. Tell him how much you miss his team and how much you want to go back.'"

I could see it all happening in front of me on the screen. Dexter's green glow was as bright as grass after a rainstorm as he whispered into Charlie's ear while Coach Benson stood in front of them. The coach clearly had no idea that Dexter was there. Charlie chewed on a knuckle, and then I heard his voice:

"No thank you, Coach Benson, I'm quite happy where I am. Coach Rudge is great. He's the best coach I've ever had, in fact!"

Dexter's green color dulled until he faded away altogether.

I stood up.

"This is utterly ridiculous! Charlie gave up baseball just because he didn't want to admit things weren't right with the new coach, *just to get back at Coach Benson*? That is the stupidest thing I've ever heard!"

Sam watched me but didn't say anything. His face was blank. He waved an arm and the image shimmered into waves and then the wall returned to normal. I threw myself back onto the sofa.

"That Charlie sounds like a complete moron. Why didn't he just say to Coach Benson—I'm sorry but, you know what, Coach Rudge isn't great. Why didn't he *tell* him? Why didn't he just tell him how bad it was?"

Sam crouched down beside me and rested his arms on his knees. He leaned forward and looked straight at me, and as he did his eyes seemed to age. The skin around them looked suddenly thinner, and wrinkles began to form. It almost felt like I was looking into my dad's eyes.

"Why didn't he just admit he was upset?" I said, in a whisper.

"I don't know, Nate," said Sam, aging before my eyes. "Why did you tell your dad that Gary was great when he wasn't?"

I shut my eyes, and when I opened them again, Sam was gone.

## CHAPTER 24
# THE BIRTHDAY

I woke up the next morning a twelve-year-old. My mum was missing, there was a scraggy chicken in the kitchen, I had a glowing imaginary friend in the living room, and somewhere outside was a weird treasure hunter named Kitty. I think it was perfectly fine that on this year, more than any other, all I wanted to do was pull the duvet over my head and stay in bed. I could hear the chicken making a squawking noise in the kitchen. Her food was probably all gone, and I knew I should go down and let her out, but I couldn't. I just couldn't get out of bed.

I felt my breath hot against my chin as I lay there. I decided I'd just stay there in bed and wait. I'd wait for time to pass and for Mum to come back and then everything would be all right. She'd walk back in with a big smile on her face.

*"I'm so sorry I was so long, Nate. I've been busy making this for you! It's taken me ages."*

From behind her back she'd reveal a huge, three-tiered birthday cake. That's what must have happened. She was just busy somewhere making a surprise cake for my birthday. Or maybe it wasn't that at all. Maybe she was back with Gary, forgetting all about my birthday, forgetting all about me.

I felt tears prickle and begin to fall—I dabbed the duvet on my cheeks, trying to soak them up, but they just kept coming.

―――――――――――

My sixth birthday had probably been my best birthday ever. Mum and Dad were still together back then, and they'd hired the village hall for a party. We turned up two hours before the guests were due, along with Grandma and Granddad, and we set about decorating the whole hall. I say "we" but it was really them. I just spent two hours running the length of the hall and skidding along on my knees until Grandma eventually told me to get up as I was ruining the nice khakis that she'd bought for me.

I'd invited twenty-two friends from school, and they all turned up at exactly three o'clock—each with a gift-wrapped present that they dumped on a big table before running around hitting one another over the head with balloons. I ran around too, but I kept an eye on the table as the mound of gifts grew and grew. I couldn't believe it—I'd never seen so many presents in my whole life.

After ten minutes of running around we were all told to sit down, as the magician, the Great Stupendo, was about to start his routine. We sat down on the floor by his feet and stared up at the large man wearing a dark robe covered in little golden stars. He started off a bit rubbish (he made a plastic birthday cake disappear, but we could all see that it folded flat and he'd just squashed it with a lid). But the tricks got better and better, and we all went crazy when he poured a jug of milk into a newspaper funnel and nothing got wet. Toward the end of his routine he asked me up to be his assistant. All I had to do was hold the magic wand while he got everything ready for the next trick. But when he gave it to me it went all floppy, like a piece of black rope. My friends burst into laughter.

"What are you doing, young man?" cried the Great Stupendo, making the wand go back to normal again. "You've just got one task! Just hold tightly onto this magic wand, and I'll get everything ready for the next trick . . ."

He turned away and the wand, which was normal in his hand, collapsed into a useless, floppy stick when I held it.

My friends went wild.

"Look! It's gone all funny!" they screamed. "He can't do magic tricks with that!"

I stood there frozen, the droopy wand hanging over my hand. I didn't understand it—what was I doing wrong?

The magician acted all flustered.

"Come on now, Nate. Stop this messing around. We've got a captive audience here, and they're waiting for the headlining trick in my act—aren't you, boys and girls?"

"Yes!"

"Okay, well don't mess it up again . . ."

He took the wand from me and gave it a wipe with his magic scarf and it miraculously went solid again.

"So, this is your last chance to get this right, Nate. You've just got one job to do, just hold this for me while I . . ."

The wand was back in my hand, and it instantly slumped across my palm as if it had fainted.

The audience was hysterical now, and Daisy Harrison had actually rolled onto her back, clutching her stomach.

But I wasn't laughing.

The magician made a great fuss and wiped at his forehead with hundreds of multicolored scarves that he pulled from his pockets. My friends were going crazy now, trying to catch the little squares as he threw them into the air.

I looked at everyone laughing at me, and then I saw Mum and Dad watching from the back of the hall. They were standing apart, both with their arms crossed. Dad was smiling at me and he gave me a quick thumbs-up, but Mum had her eyes fixed on the magician. She began to make her way around the kids sitting on the floor, edging toward the front. She stopped to one side for a moment as she bit on the end of her nail. She does that when she's thinking.

The Great Stupendo took the wand again, which magically returned to its proper shape. I had one eye on the wand and one eye on Mum. This could be a disaster; she was going to show me up in front of *everyone*.

"I'd normally give up by now, young Nate. But as it's your birthday I'll give you one more try. It's quite simple. All you have to do, my little fellow, is hold onto this very, very precious wand that was carved from wood from Outer Mongolia. Can you do that for me?"

I nodded.

He held the black wand up in front of my face, took my hand, and placed it firmly on my palm. I heard a little click and the wand sagged onto my palm again, just as Mum took a step forward. The screams of laughter were ear piercing.

"You've done something to it!" I shouted. "I heard it!" I turned toward the crowd. "There was a little click—it isn't my fault it's not working. He made it go like that!"

The laughter faded as all the children stared at me. Daisy Harrison pushed herself up off the floor, her mouth open with shock. They couldn't believe that the birthday boy was ruining the whole act.

The Great Stupendo patted me firmly on the shoulder. "Now, now, there's no need for that. You don't want to spoil it for everyone, do you? Maybe one of your other guests would like to be my assistant instead?"

Twenty arms shot up instantly. I threw the wand onto the floor and made a run for the bathroom.

"Nate! Wait!" called Mum and I could hear her running across the hall behind me. She caught me before I could get to the boys' room. "What was all that about? It was just a trick."

"You were going to say something. You were going to embarrass me in front of all of my friends!"

Dad appeared behind her. "I think you've done a good job of that yourself, don't you?" he said. I ignored them both and ran into the bathroom, locking myself in a stall. They must have decided to leave me to it, as no one followed.

After about fifteen minutes of hiding, Eddie Durrant came in and found me standing by the sinks with my arms folded. His face was dripping with sweat.

"What're you doing in here? You're missing your own party!" he said, splashing his face with some cold water. "It's mad in there. Your dad's got us all doing a giant conga. Come on!"

He rushed back to the hall, and I slowly followed him out. Someone had turned the big lights off, and the bright disco lights were swirling around the hall as a snake of kids wound its way this way and that. My dad was at the front with a party hat on his head, laughing and kicking his legs.

"Nate! Grab me!" said Malaya Barnes, who swept past me at the end of the line. I ran and placed my hands on her shoulders and grinned as I kicked a leg to one side and then to the other.

After the last person had left and we'd swept the hall and turned off the lights I remember climbing exhausted into the back of the car. The trunk was stuffed with presents ready to open when I got home. Mum turned around to me:

"Happy birthday, darling. I hope you've had a lovely party," she said, smiling.

I grinned back at her.

"Thank you, Mum. It's been the best day ever."

———————————

I'd forgotten all about my tantrum in the middle of the party. I'd felt like such an idiot up there with that magician, being laughed at by everyone, but I was more worried that Mum was going to wade in and make me look even more stupid. It was funny, but I'd always imagined that that day had been the best day of my life. I guess even good ones can't be all perfect. Mum must have been so upset with me for spoiling everything, but she never mentioned it once.

I shut my eyes, trying to go back to sleep, but the room was too bright and my eyelids glowed yellow.

"You getting up then?"

I squinted. At the end of my bed was Sam, his bright T-shirt glowing like a hazy sun.

"Go away," I said, and I shut my eyes again. I could sense him walking around to the side of my bed.

"Nate, it's your birthday. And there's a whole bunch of people downstairs who have traveled quite a way to meet you. So just get yourself up and come see. Okay?"

I opened my eyes, but he'd left. I lay there for a moment, listening to the sounds of the cottage creaking and the wind rustling through the trees outside, and then I rolled over and shut my eyes again.

After about a minute I could hear singing. It was distant but it was definitely there. I sat up and listened.

*"For he's a jolly good fellow, for he's a jolly good fellow . . . for he's a jolly good felllooooowww . . . and so say all of us . . ."*

Then there was lots of clapping and cheering. What was going on?

I got out of bed, pulled a sweater over my pajamas, and slowly walked to the top of the stairs. The noises were getting louder. It sounded like there was a crowd of people in the living room.

"Is he coming?"

"Are you sure you haven't just imagined him, Sam?"

"When's he coming? When can we meet him?"

I slowly walked down the stairs. The living room door was shut, but I could see lights coming from the gap at the bottom. Bright lights. I held the handle and slowly turned it.

"SURPRISE!"

I stumbled backward, dazzled by the colors that filled the room. It was packed—there were imaginary friends everywhere. I held my hand up and used the wall to steady myself as I took it all in. Sam appeared in front of me, his grin wide and his yellow T-shirt brighter than ever.

"Happy birthday, Nate!" he said.

I just stared at him, openmouthed.

"Come and meet everyone!"

A girl wearing silver-framed glasses and a silver sweater and jeans pushed through the crowd and jumped in front of us.

"Hi, I'm Beth. Happy birthday! Great to see you."

She gave me a little wave, and I held up my hand and gave a feeble wiggle of my fingers.

"Are you for real?" said another girl, pushing through the crowd. She was wearing a pair of bright orange overalls. When she got closer her eyes widened. "Wow, Sam. You *were* telling the truth after all! He *is* real."

"Well, of course I'm real . . ." I said, but no one was listening.

"Nate! Nate! Over here!"

In the corner behind the mass of figures were Meena and Dexter, the imaginary friends from Sam's stories. Meena was waving her arms about and Sam began to edge toward them, so I followed. As I passed, the friends all stared at me, grinning madly. Some even bowed.

"It's so nice to see you!"

"Isn't he amazing? I can't believe he's really here."

"And on a special day like today. His very own birthday!"

I smiled at them as I went, unable to speak.

Meena was jumping up and down, clapping her hands.

"So, what do you think?" she said. "Is this the best birthday you've ever had, or what?!"

I opened my mouth to reply, but nothing came out.

"The guy is overwhelmed, aren't you, Nate?" said Dexter. "Come on, let's get the music on!"

From somewhere, I don't know where or how, music began to play. It began with a rhythmic drumbeat, and then a man started singing about sun shining in the sky. I knew it immediately; it was "Mr. Blue Sky," my mum's favorite song ever. I felt tears prickling my eyes.

"Come on, Nate! Let's dance!" squealed Meena, and she leapt into action and shimmied this way and that along with the other figures. I looked around and *everyone* was dancing: Some jumped up and down in time to the repetitive beat, some shook their heads, and some held on to each other and spun around and around. It was like watching an incredible, swirling rainbow right there in the living room. I stood still for a moment, and then I caught the eye of the girl in the orange overalls, who was waving her arms above her head. She made her way over to me, and I wiped the tears away from my cheeks.

"Come on, Nate! It's your birthday! Dance!"

I gave her a smile and took a deep breath. She was right. It was my birthday! I shrugged and then I went for it. I jumped about and sang the words as loudly as I could. Everyone began whooping and clapping around me, and I danced and danced until I could barely breathe. I hopped onto the sofa, and everyone cheered as I pogoed up and down, laughing. Some of the others joined me, and someone climbed onto the armchair and did some sort of weird break dancing. We danced and we danced until I was sweating and out of breath. The music grew louder and louder until it slowed right down. Sounds of violins and a piano filled the room, and all of the friends slowed and swayed gently until the music came to a steady end with the words . . .

"*Mr. Blue Sky . . . y . . .*"

I stopped and looked around me, breathless and silent. Then they all erupted into cheers.

"Happy birthday, Nate! You are the best!"

I nodded and smiled and took a bow, turning around in a slow circle. As I did I spotted a boy standing on his own in the corner. He was a lot younger than the rest of them, and he was wearing gray and chewing on the cuff of his sweater. His eyes were fixed on the floor. Sam was standing beside me.

"Who's he?" I asked.

"That's Arthur," said Sam.

"Why is he so . . . pale? Why isn't he in color like the rest of you?"

Sam looked sad.

"He didn't complete his time as an imaginary."

I watched Arthur looking uncomfortable.

"What do you mean?" I said.

"Most of our real friends just stop seeing us one day, once they've reached the right age. It's almost as if they've forgotten we were there in the first place and they just don't need us any more. For Arthur, and for some of the others, it's different."

I watched as the pale gray boy looked nervously around the room. "What do you mean, different?"

Sam thought for a moment. I could tell he was finding it hard to talk about, and he was trying to find the right words.

"Sometimes it can't be helped. Sometimes your life as an imaginary friend comes to an abrupt ending that is out of anyone's control."

I swallowed. "How do you mean?"

Sam leaned closer toward me.

"If your friend dies," he whispered. I hugged myself tightly.

I looked back at the fading boy. He sniffed, then wiped his nose on his sleeve and stared straight at me through his bangs. He looked so sad.

"What happens to him now?" I said.

Sam shrugged. "He's supposed to find another friend, but he refuses. He doesn't want to let go of his responsibilities to his old one. He needs to let go first. *Then* he can move on."

I wanted to go over and talk to him, but a boy in a suit the shade of a tropical ocean jumped in my way. "Nate! Nate! Read to us from your *Freaky Things* book!" he said.

"Yes, go on, Nate!" called a girl by the fire. Everyone parted and made room for me as I walked toward the sofa. My *Freaky Things* book was lying on the floor, the pages bent back on themselves.

"Tell us one of your best freaky facts. Are there any about birds? I love birds," said a girl in an outfit the color of rubies. She sat down on the floor, waiting.

"And make it a funny one!" shouted Dexter from across the room.

I picked up the book and straightened the creased pages as I looked at the eager faces around me—all apart from Arthur, who was still standing in his gray corner. I hesitated as I watched to see if he was going to join in, but he didn't move, so I sat down and began.

"Right, okay . . . Let me see," I said as I flicked through the book. "I think I know the exact one."

I found the page I wanted, and then I cleared my throat and began.

"In Papua New Guinea there lives a bird of extreme rarity. This bird of paradise is called the resplendent iris bird, and it is the only species in existence to . . ."

I paused for comic effect.

". . . have multicolored poos."

The entire room gasped.

"Scientists believe that this colorful poo occurs because of the bird's bright plumage."

I grinned and turned the book around so they could see the illustration of a bird covered in feathers of every color imaginable. It had its head cocked to one side, and next to it was a pile of brightly colored poo. There was a second of silence, and then the whole room erupted into fits of laughter.

"Look! It's made a pile of rainbow!" squealed a boy in pastel peach, clutching his stomach.

"That is amazing," said a girl in dark emerald green. "I've never seen anything like that before."

I grinned as everyone crowded around me, trying to take a look at my book. The only one who didn't move was the boy in gray, his face pale against his washed-out sweater. He hung back in the corner, looking over now and then as if he wanted to join in but couldn't. I gave him a smile, and he quickly looked away.

"Let's get some more music on!" shouted Dexter, and everyone cheered. A steady drum began to thud, and I shimmied my shoulders left and right in time to the beat. The imaginary friends around me did the same, watching me for the next move. I was leading some kind of bizarre group dance. I laughed as I spun around and they all did the same, trying to keep up with me as the music swirled around us. We laughed and we jumped and we kicked, but as the song came to an end I noticed some of the friends began to fade. I spun around and around, and when I got back to the middle there were fewer friends. Eventually all of the colors in the room evaporated and it was back to its dark, dull self. I stood panting in the middle of the room. I was all alone again.

# CHAPTER 25

# THE MAZE

After everyone had gone I felt so empty.

I curled up on the sofa and squeezed my eyes shut. I wondered what would happen if I just stayed here. I'd let the sofa slowly swallow me up, becoming just another lump among its many bulges and springs. They'd find me in a few weeks, I imagined. Maybe they'd interview Kitty and she'd tell the police how she took me on a treasure hunt around the grounds of her mansion.

I screwed my eyes tighter, and then I heard a noise coming from the kitchen. I looked up as Kitty walked in, horror on her face. "You do realize there's a chicken in here, don't you?" she said.

"I—I thought it . . . I just thought she might have been cold out there in this weather, so . . ."

Kitty raised her eyebrows. She was acting strange, looking around the room suspiciously.

"Were you singing just now?" she said, folding her arms. "I thought I could hear someone singing?"

I looked at her and shook my head, and she stared back at me.

"Nate, you're on your own here, aren't you?"

I could feel my throat tense. I'm pretty sure she'd guessed a while ago, but it was still hard to admit it.

"No. My parents are just out . . . They'll be back soon . . . I just . . ."

"Nate, you said your parents aren't together anymore. There's no need to make stuff up. Not to me anyway. Are you on your own?"

I hung my head and closed my eyes and I nodded.

She bit her lip, her face frowning as she thought about it, and then she suddenly clapped her hands together. "Right, you get the fire going, and I'll see what I can find for breakfast. That chicken of yours has laid a couple of eggs by the back door, so you could boil them up, maybe?"

She turned back to the kitchen without waiting for an answer. I curled up on the sofa again and began to cry. Silently at first, but then the tears came really fast and I couldn't stop. I hugged myself and I sobbed until my stomach hurt. I wanted to tell her it was my birthday today, that I was all alone and that I'd thought my mum was missing but now I was sure she'd gone back to her boyfriend. Her nasty, angry, horrible boyfriend. But I couldn't say any of those things, so I just cried.

"You lighting that fire yet?" called Kitty from the kitchen. "Come on. We've got the maze to solve today. And you need to eat something first."

I wiped my eyes with my sleeve and pushed myself up, and then I knelt down beside the fire and opened the little glass door.

We sat at the dining table, and I ate my boiled egg. I'd found an eggcup in the back of the cupboard that was in the shape of an astronaut's suit—the egg made it look like it had a head and a helmet. I smashed the top with a little spoon and ate the warm, runny yolk in silence. I didn't know how long it would be before she told someone that I was here on my own. An hour? A day? I kept glancing at her, trying to work out what was going through her head, but she was just absorbed in studying the map of the house and the grounds. If she told the authorities, then someone would come and get me and naturally they'd just take me back to my address. To Gary. They'd probably assume that Mum and Gary had had an argument and that she had gone off in a huff and had left me uncared for. Or maybe Gary had tracked Mum down and was keeping her prisoner at home. Or maybe they were there together and they'd say they didn't want me? I couldn't think about that. It was too painful.

"Look! This map shows how the maze is built," said Kitty, and she held up the plans. Because they were from an aerial position, they showed exactly which way we needed to go to get to the middle.

"It might not be any good now though. It's so overgrown. But we should take that with us anyway," I said.

I finished my egg and folded up the large plans the best I could, with the maze part at the front so I didn't have to unfold the whole thing again.

Kitty hadn't mentioned me being on my own anymore, but I was waiting for it. I tried a distraction. "Did you have a cook at home?"

Kitty blinked at me for a moment and then nodded.

"We used to. Mrs. Kemp—that was the cook—but she's been gone for a while now. Years. They all have."

"All?" I said. "Did you have lots of people working there?"

Kitty nodded and smiled. "Oh yes, there was a groom, house-keepers, William the gardener of course, and a chauffeur. There were fresh flowers delivered every Friday. They'd be put in a great big vase on the table in the entrance hall so that when guests came, they'd be the first thing seen."

She stood up.

"Right. You'd better get dressed. We've got a maze to solve!"

I headed to the stairs and she called after me.

"And put on some extra layers. The snow is really thick out there."

I looked out the window beside the front door. She was right, a few more centimeters must have fallen overnight; you couldn't see the road at all. Everywhere looked so pretty and unspoiled. It would be the first white birthday I'd ever had. And the first without my mum.

I found some old shopping bags in a kitchen drawer and put them over my sneakers so that my feet didn't get wet in the snow. I felt like an idiot and they were a bit slippery to walk in, but I couldn't imagine we'd bump into anyone. And if we did, plastic bags on my feet were the least of my problems.

We walked through the wood in silence, apart from my rustling feet. It was odd that Kitty hadn't mentioned me being on my own. It was as if she wasn't shocked at all, or maybe she just didn't care? Either way I decided I should probably say something.

"Look, I just want to say it's no big deal about me being here on my own. I'm just waiting . . . for my mum to come back. Okay? She just had to go and . . . do some stuff . . . But no one can know I'm here."

Kitty shrugged. "Okay."

"Okay?" I said. I was expecting her to say more. "Seriously. If anyone knows I'm here, then it could be bad for me. Really, really bad."

Kitty looked worried for a minute. I knew I was asking a lot from her, to keep quiet about this.

"One of your shopping bags is coming off," she said, nodding her head down toward my feet.

I quickly tucked the bag back into my sock as she walked on. I could probably trust her not to say anything straightaway—after all, she needed me to help solve the treasure hunt—but I didn't think she'd keep it a secret for too long.

We came to the entrance of the maze, and Kitty took a deep breath.

"Right. Let's look at the map," I said, getting the folded plans out of my pocket. I studied the route.

"It looks like we have to turn right first, and then it's just a matter of counting the paths and taking the third one and then the second one and then the first one, then back to the third. I think that's right."

"Great," she said, and she grinned, putting her satchel over her head and across her body.

"You ready?"

I nodded.

"Right! Let's go and find this treasure!" she said.

She pulled her hat a little lower, then brushed past the branches and disappeared into the maze. I pushed in behind her and made my way along the overgrown, narrow tunnel. The branches scratched at my face, and I came to the end and looked left and right. Kitty was nowhere to be seen. Had she rushed off alone? What was I supposed to do? Go on without her? I stood there for a moment, and then her pale face appeared through the shrubbery.

"This way!" she said and she turned right.

I pulled a twig out of my ear and folded my arms, tucking my hands away so they didn't get scratched, and then followed her.

We counted each path, took a left, then counted two and turned right.

"So, we need to take the first path next. Is that right?" I said, looking at the map again.

Kitty nodded, but she looked just as confused as me. We carried on, but then we came to a sort of crossroads. It was hard to tell because it was so overgrown. I looked at the map again, but I couldn't work out where we were.

"Let's just go straight on," she said and headed forward. I followed behind her as she twisted and turned through the maze, barely looking up.

"Hang on, Kitty. Aren't we just going in circles? We must have gone wrong somewhere."

I rubbed my forehead.

"Where now?" she said.

"Hold on, I'm thinking."

I looked behind us at the mass of green branches, then looked ahead and left and right and then back at the map. Everything seemed the same. I had no idea.

"I think we should go back the way we came and take a different path," I said.

We turned around and went back. I looked up and could see that it was starting to snow again, a few flakes managing to get through the thick greenery. We got back to a crossroads and this time we headed off in a different direction.

"Have you decided what you are going to do when you've found the treasure?" I asked.

Kitty smiled. "I don't know. It's exciting though, isn't it? I wonder what it'll be! I bet it's something special, for Charlotte."

"Your dad will be pleased. Have you told him you're doing this? That you've been trying to solve the treasure hunt."

Kitty shook her head. "No, he doesn't know."

She turned left and then immediately took a path to the right.

"And what if it's nothing? What if there is no treasure, Kitty? What will you do?"

She frowned and then snickered.

"Don't be ridiculous. Of course there is going to be something." She laughed. "Can you imagine going to all this trouble just for there *not* to be anything at the end of it? I mean, what a waste of time that would be! No, there's going to be something, and it's going to be big. William has left something a-maze-ing, I just know it. Get it? A-maze-ing?" She laughed again.

"Yeah, Kitty. I get it," I said. I was about to say something about her being prepared, in case she was wrong, but I could see the hope in her face, so I kept quiet. I'd be leaving soon, and I had no idea how things were going to go for me. I just hoped things would work out for her.

We twisted and turned and doubled back on ourselves two more times before we finally emerged into a square, open clearing.

"Is this it? Are we in the middle?" I said. We seemed to have reached it more by accident than planning.

"It must be," said Kitty as she walked out into the thicker snow. In the center was a low concrete column. Kitty ran over and brushed the snow away using her arm.

"What is it?" I asked. "Is it a sundial?"

I looked at the concrete plinth. It looked familiar. In fact, the center of the maze looked familiar.

"I don't think it's a sundial. Look, it's completely flat."

The top of the column was covered with a metal plate, and inscribed in it were lots of lines and dots. Some of the dots were tiny and some were larger circles. I suddenly recognized some of the shapes.

"It's a celestial map!" I said.

"A what?" said Kitty, studying the tiny bumps.

"A celestial map. A map of the stars. Look, there's Cassiopeia, and that's Taurus." I traced the dots with my finger. "This is a map of all the major star constellations."

"You know about everything, don't you?!"

I shrugged, but it was all because of my book, *Freaky Things*. There were four whole pages dedicated to star constellations, and I'd learned them all and compared them to the night sky. I knew I was right.

Lines joined the dots together, showing the constellations' shapes. Kitty crouched over and studied it.

"Let me read the riddle again," I said. "There was something about being up on high, wasn't there?"

Kitty quickly took the clue out of her coat pocket.

*A huntsman bright am I, I watch from up on high. By day I can't be seen, you'll find me boxed in green.*

"Yes! This is starting to make sense now!" I said, but Kitty still looked blank.

"So, the 'boxed in green' bit I get—that's the maze because the hedge is called a box," she said. "What else have we got?"

"'I watch from up on high'—it must be a star constellation. And we all know which one relates to a huntsman. It's easy! I can't believe I missed it!"

I grinned at her, but she just shook her head. "Nope. You've got to give me more here."

I pointed at the map. "Orion! He was a great hunter. Look, there's his belt." I traced the three dots on the cold metal as Kitty watched. "He looks over the Pleiades. That's another group of stars."

Kitty looked at me blankly, and then she looked around the map.

"Well, where is he then?" she asked. She felt the edges of the metal sheet to see if she could lever it off.

I looked around the middle of the maze, but there wasn't anything else here.

"Kitty, those statues that you've got outside your house. Are you sure none of them look like a hunter?"

Kitty frowned and shook her head. "No. And why would he lead us here to then send us off somewhere else without another clue? He said 'find me boxed in green,' so it must be here. It must be in the maze!"

She crouched back down and looked underneath the map at the stone column.

"Nate, look at this," she said.

I knelt down beside her. The four sides of the column had carvings. Each one showed a constellation in more detail, with the drawing of what it represented around it. The first was of Cassiopeia, with a woman wearing some grand clothing, the next side was of the Great Bear, then there was one I thought was Perseus of a man etched around his stars, and finally there was Orion, holding his shield up high.

"Look," I said. "This is the hunter. That's Orion. I remember now. I've been here! I have been in the middle of the maze with my parents!"

Kitty glared at me, but I grinned back at her.

"Mum said we came here years ago, but I was so young I don't really remember it. I remember being on Dad's shoulders and walking across some posh lawns. I didn't know where we were going, but now I do! We came into the maze!"

Kitty studied the base of the column.

"Look!" I said. "There's a piece of stone that's loose."

Beneath the carving of Orion was a triangle of rock that was propped against the column. The snow had nearly covered it. I pulled it away and revealed a dark little hole.

Kitty gasped.

"Is there anything in there? Have a look, Nate!"

I carefully reached inside, and my hands touched something soft. I flinched, then slowly put my hand back and brought out a small brown parcel.

"I don't believe it. We've found it, Nate! We've found the treasure. Oh my."

It was faded and a bit crumpled up and had obviously been there for a while. On the front it said *Charlotte's Treasure* in the same handwriting as the clues.

"This is it, Nate. This really is it! I've found it at last."

I held it toward her, but she shook her head.

"I can't . . . Can you open it?"

I frowned. "Shouldn't you give it to your dad?"

Kitty shook her head. "Please, Nate. Just open it?"

I tore the edge of the paper and took out some white tissue paper, and then I carefully unfolded the edges to reveal what was inside. It was a tiny rocking horse carved out of wood.

Kitty gasped. "A rocking horse! He made her a rocking horse for her dollhouse."

I held it up. Kitty was enthralled, and her eyes were shining bright blue. It was as if we'd found the most precious thing in the world.

"Charlotte loved her dollhouse. She loved it so much. I can't believe he made this for her!"

Kitty looked overwhelmed by it all. I went to give the rocking horse to her, but she shook her head again.

"No. I don't want it. I think you should . . . I think you should put it back."

I was stunned.

"Put it back? After all the trouble you've been to?"

Kitty nodded.

"Yes, it should stay here. Definitely."

At first I thought it was a bit silly to go to all this trouble to find the prize to then put it back again. But then, it wasn't Kitty's—it was Charlotte's—so perhaps leaving it here was the right thing to do. I carefully wrapped it back up and placed it back in the hole, beneath the carving of Orion.

I stood up and brushed the wet snow from my jeans.

"Thank you for doing this, Nate. Thank you for doing this for me. And for Charlotte."

I shrugged. "It's okay."

We started to walk back through the maze.

"It's only a small thing, but a gift like that would have meant so much to her, I'm sure."

Even though this family didn't mean anything to me, I could see that the present from William was a lovely thing to do.

We walked for a while in silence. We'd been so busy finding Charlotte's treasure that I'd forgotten all about it being my birthday. And Charlotte wasn't the only one with a gift. Mum's present to me was still waiting in her bag, in her bedroom. My heart fluttered. She'd brought me a birthday present, and now I could open it.

# CHAPTER 26

# FINDING THE WAY

It took us ages to get out of the maze. Kitty kept asking me why the rush, but I just said I needed to get back to the cottage. As soon as we emerged from the entrance I yelled goodbye and sprinted as fast as I could across the snow.

The chicken was sitting on the back doorstep, and she squawked when I rushed inside, my wet feet skidding on the kitchen floor. I ran up to Mum's room and grabbed the bag, which I'd emptied apart from the one thing. I sat on her bed and slowly undid the zipper. There it was, nestling in the corner as if it had been waiting for me all this time. My birthday gift. My birthday gift from my mum. I carefully undid the sticky tape, and beneath the blue polka-dot wrapping paper were layers and layers of yellow tissue, protecting whatever was inside. I unpeeled them one by one, my hands trembling, and then finally, there it was.

My present.

It was a light jar.

The most beautiful light jar I had ever seen. My heart pounded as I unscrewed the silver lid and took out the little bunch of lights. I found the switch and clicked it on and the tiny bulbs twinkled against the glass. It looked magical.

I took a deep breath.

Mum wouldn't have gotten this for me if she was going to go back to Gary. No way. This present was her way of telling me we were going to have a fresh start, without him. I felt relief. Relief that I'd been wrong about her. Relief that she hadn't gone back to him after all. But then my heart sank. If she wasn't with Gary, where was she? There must be another reason for her not coming back.

Something must have happened to her.

I filled my backpack with my *Freaky Things* book, Mrs. Ellie-Fant, the Ask Me a Question magic ball, my tennis ball, and all the other things I'd brought with me. I put my light jar on top and closed the zipper. I had to get help. I had to find out what had happened to my mum.

As I packed, I came up with a plan. I was going to go to the big house and ask Kitty's family for help. I'd say I was a friend of Kitty's and could I possibly use their telephone. Kitty's parents would probably be a bit shocked when I appeared on their doorstep; they might even be a little angry, not knowing who I was, but they couldn't refuse to help. Could they? Then I'd call Grandma and tell her everything. And then I was going to ask Grandma the big question. When we find Mum, could we come and live with her?

I found two more plastic shopping bags, and I sat on the sofa and put them on over my sneakers, tucking the tops into my socks.

"So, you're off then? Not going to say goodbye?"

Sam had appeared beside me. I stopped for a moment, then carried on sorting out my footwear. My feet rustled as I moved.

"There's no need. You can turn up whenever you want to, so why say goodbye? I'll see you when I'm at Grandma's."

I couldn't look at him. Not yet.

"We both know we won't see each other again, Nate," said Sam. I took a deep breath and this time I looked up at him.

"I thought seeing you was my choice? You've always said it was because of me that you were here in the first place. That means if I want to see you again, then I will, won't I?"

Sam smiled. "But you don't need me any more. There's a difference."

I felt my cheeks burning. "B-But you'd love it at Grandma's. She's got the most amazing garden! We could play hot potato with the tennis ball or hide-and-seek or whatever you fancy."

I stopped. Sam's face was telling me it was no use.

"I can't, Nate. It's time for me to go."

Tears ran down my cheeks.

"I need you, Sam, okay? I know, I know that I haven't always been the best of friends to you . . . B-But I don't want to be on my own. I don't want to be on my own ever again."

Sam smiled. His color was bright. As bright as it was when I'd first seen him back when I was small.

"I can't stay, Nate. You need to do this alone, okay? You need to find help and you need to do it for you."

He looked away and stared toward the corner of the room where he'd disappeared before, and then he took a step toward it.

"No, no, no! I'm not ready!" I called. "I—I want to tell you things! Show you more of the things in my book. You haven't seen them all yet, have you? There are so many wonderful things in the world, Sam. Did you know that? Did you know how many amazing things are out there? I can tell you all about them!"

I was sobbing now, but I didn't care. I just didn't want him to leave.

"You're my best friend, Sam. You're my very best friend. And you're everything *I* want to be."

Sam stopped in the corner and turned around to face me. "But, Nate, I *am* you."

I stopped crying, trying to get my breath back. "What? What do you mean?"

He smiled again.

"I'm right there." He lifted his arm and pointed toward my face. His color was so bright now it dazzled my eyes. "I've been there with you all along."

And then he gave me a final smile before turning away and vanishing into the corner.

I shivered. The room was cold and dim, and he wasn't going to be coming back ever, ever again. I rubbed at my face. He was gone.

And I was all alone again.

———————————

The chicken was sitting in her washing-up bowl. I scrunched up some stale cornflakes and filled a bowl and then topped up her water. I couldn't leave her shut inside, so I left the kitchen door open a little so she could go out and then come in for shelter when she wanted. I gently tickled the top of her head on the soft feathers.

"Bye, chicken," I said. "Thanks for the eggs."

I took one last look around the empty kitchen, and then I stepped out into the snow.

# CHAPTER 27

# THE BIG HOUSE

It was snowing heavily. My footprints from earlier were nearly gone, and I left fresh, deep prints as I made my way to William's Gate for the last time. Once I'd walked through the old iron gate I picked up my pace and quickly made my way across the woodland floor, leaving a trail of trodden-down snow behind me. I got to the edge of the woods and looked up. All I needed to do was to head around the back of the maze, across the lawns toward William's sheds, and then up to the house.

I sprinted the best I could, but it was hard in the thick snow, especially with plastic bags over my shoes. My breath steamed from my mouth like an old train, and I couldn't feel my feet properly.

I stopped by some old brambles to get my breath back. The great gray house stared at me from across the patio. Nothing moved at all, apart from the flurries teeming from the sky. The blue sheeting that covered one of the holes in the roof had now turned completely white. The whole house looked frozen—like it was captured in a mighty snow globe.

I quickly walked on and headed around the side to the front of the house and looked up. The gray-bricked walls loomed over me. There were hardly any clear windows left at all around this side; most of them were boarded up. Seven steps led to a large door that was crusty with peeling black paint, and I slowly climbed them and then lifted a large brass knocker. It thudded loudly against the wood, the sound echoing inside, and then I took a step back and waited.

Nothing.

I lifted the knocker again and gave three deep bangs. I stood there for a few minutes, but no one came. Maybe there was another door I could try? I walked along the house and peered in through one of the large windows, holding my hands up to shield my eyes. The room was dark and dusty, with a grand old marble fireplace at one end. The wallpaper had peeled away like it had been cut with a knife. There was a small pile of rubble in the middle of the room, and when I looked up I could see that part of the ceiling had fallen in. This must be the area of the house that Kitty's family didn't use any more. She'd said some of the building had been closed off, so maybe they didn't use the door I'd knocked on, which would explain why no one had answered.

I carried on along the house, then turned left around the side. Every now and then I looked in through the dirty glass, but the rooms were all the same: dark and empty with crumbling walls. Some had bare electric wires hanging out of the ceiling. I stopped to look at one room and saw that a section of the floor was missing and there was just a gaping black hole in the middle. And in the corner was an old brown dollhouse. It had four floors and the front had partly fallen off, but I could see inside was a jumble of miniature furniture and cobwebs.

"I don't believe it. That must be Charlotte's dollhouse," I said, my breath steaming up the glass of the window. "That must be what the rocking horse was for."

I shivered. Something wasn't right. I knew the house needed work, but surely there would be some sign of Kitty's family? I spotted a doorway up ahead and hurried toward it. This must have been the door the servants would have used in the old days. It wasn't as big as the one at the front, and there were no grand steps up to it. Or a knocker. My heart was racing. This must be it. This must be the door the family used. I made a fist and hit my knuckles hard against the wood. Within seconds I heard footsteps and the door opened.

A man wearing a bright, luminous orange jacket and a yellow hard hat was standing in front of me. "Can I help you?"

I froze. This must be James Turner-Wright, Kitty's father. But why was he wearing a hard hat? He had a clipboard under his arm.

"I—I'm a friend of Kitty's," I said.

The man raised his eyebrows, then looked down at the plastic bags on my feet. "Sorry. Who?"

I coughed. "Kitty. I wondered if I . . . erm . . . if I could please use your telephone, sir?"

The man in the yellow hat snorted. "Kitty? Sorry, son, but there's no Kitty here. No one has lived in this place for about . . . oh, fifty years?"

My throat tightened. I reached a hand to the side and held on to the cold, frozen wall.

"I—I . . . What did you say?" I stammered.

"I'm from the health and safety department, and I'm here today to assess the place before any work commences. You must have the wrong house. Have you checked the address?"

My ears started to ring. This wasn't making sense. It wasn't making sense at all. "B-But what about Kitty?"

The man frowned at me. "This Kitty . . . She wouldn't have anything to do with a car that's parked halfway down the driveway, would she? Looks like it's been abandoned."

I shook my head.

"What? No. She's about my age. She lives here with her mum and dad. Kitty Turner-Wright. She's a bit shorter than me. Wears a blue woolly hat."

The health and safety man gave a low chuckle. "There's no one here called Kitty, I promise you. Are you sure you haven't imagined her?"

I felt like I was going to be sick. No. She couldn't be . . . I looked behind the man, trying to see inside the house. There was a staircase in the center of the hall, but most of the steps were missing. I began to shout.

"Kitty? Kitty! It's me, it's Nate!"

I tried to get around him, but he was blocking the way. "I'm sorry, son, but you can't come in here. It's not safe," he said, holding his arms out wide.

It didn't make sense. She couldn't be . . . She couldn't. I took a few steps backward and shouted her name with all my might.

"KITTY!"

# CHAPTER 28

# LOOKING FOR KITTY

I ran away from the health and safety man and around the side of the house.

"Kitty! Kitty! Where are you?" I shouted, looking through the cracked windows.

"Come back!" said the man, skidding and sliding behind me. "I haven't checked around there—it might not be safe!"

But he was too slow. I turned a corner and spotted a door that was open and quickly ducked inside. I stood still for a moment and heard the health and safety man run past. My eyes adjusted to the gloom, and I looked around. I was in a kitchen. There were cupboards all around the outside, and a lot of them had doors missing.

I felt sick. All I kept seeing was Kitty's face as she stood grinning at me in the woods. Her woolly hat pulled low over her eyebrows. Her brown satchel slung over her shoulder. Her lips turning blue from the cold. Where was she? It didn't make any sense.

"Kitty!" I called. "Kitty, are you in here?"

I walked through the kitchen and came out into a hallway. To the left was a staircase.

"Hello! Kitty! Where are you?"

"Help!"

A voice cried out from somewhere deep in the house. *"Help me!"*

I ran toward the stairs. "I'm coming! Kitty, I'm coming!"

I got to the stairs and stopped. There was a hole in the ground just where the first step should have been. A great, gaping hole like I'd seen through the other windows. The floor must have collapsed.

"Is there someone there? Help me . . . please!"

I lay on my stomach and peered over the edge, the floorboards creaking beneath me. I could see a shape. It was a person lying on their side, down in the hole.

"Kitty? Kitty, are you there?" I called into the darkness.

And then a voice called out to me. A voice I knew. A voice I'd missed so very much.

"Nate? Nate, is that you?"

I blinked into the deep, black hole. "Mum?"

And then someone grabbed my ankles.

# CHAPTER 29

# COLIN

"It's all right. I've gotcha," said a man, and I felt myself being dragged on my stomach, away from the hole in the floor.

"No! It's my mum! My mum is down there! I've got to help her!"

I spun around and faced the health and safety man. He held tightly on to my arms.

"It's all right, we will help her. But you ain't going to be any help if you fall in as well, are you?"

I sat there, stunned, as the man got down on his hands and knees and crawled toward the hole. "Hello? Hello, can you hear me? My name's Colin. Are you okay?"

I could hear coughing. My mum was coughing.

"I think . . . I think I've broken . . . I've broken my leg . . . I fell through the floor. I fell through . . . I'm so cold . . . I need water . . ."

Her voice sounded strange. The words were slurring into each other.

"You just sit tight and we'll get help. Don't you move and don't you panic. We'll get you out of there!"

Colin edged away and then he fumbled in a pocket of his bright, fluorescent jacket.

"My son! Nate! Nate, are you there?"

I stood up and Colin put his hand on my shoulder, making sure I didn't go any closer.

"I'm here, Mum. I'm fine!" I shouted.

"I'm going to take your boy outside where it's safer, and I'll phone for help. I'll be right back, I promise!"

I shook the man's hand away. "No! I'm not going anywhere."

Mum coughed again. "Nate, do as he says. Please . . ." And her voice faded away.

Colin held my arm and we walked back outside as he called an ambulance. He then got a bottle of water and some cookies from his car and grabbed a thick coat from the back seat.

"Right, you sit in my car and keep warm. I'm going to go and drop these down to your mum, and I'm going to keep her talking until help gets here. Okay?"

I studied Colin's face carefully. He looked a bit flustered, but I could tell he was doing his best. And he had kind eyes. I nodded. And then he shut the car door and I waited.

---

Everything went a bit crazy after they rescued Mum. I opened the car door to try to see what was going on, but a police officer told me to wait there. She sat with me for a while, telling me my mum was going to be fine and that they'd phoned my grandma, who was on her way. Eventually the paramedics appeared, carrying Mum on a stretcher. I could see a silver foil blanket over her and some other red ones on top of that. I didn't care what the policewoman said—I dove out of the car.

"Mum! Mum? Are you okay?" I said, running over to the stretcher.

The paramedic had placed a small plastic mask over her face. I could see she had blood running down her cheek. Her eyes were shut. She looked so cold and pale.

"Mum! Mum, it's me!"

One of the paramedics put an arm on my shoulder and was talking to me, but I couldn't hear what they were saying. I just wanted my mum to open her eyes.

"Mum! Wake up!"

# CHAPTER 30
# LOOKING FOR FIREWOOD

The hospital smelled of coffee and disinfectant. I sat on a plastic chair beside the nurse's desk and waited for Grandma to come back. She'd gone to the vending machine to get a cup of tea. There was a large swinging door and people kept coming and going back and forth, back and forth, and every time it opened I looked up to see if it was her or not. I was a bit nervous that she wasn't going to come back.

I got my *Freaky Things* book out of my backpack and found the checklist about survival. I was trying to work out if Mum would have had everything she needed:

1) Shelter

2) Water

3) Food

4) Fire

5) Attitude

She would have only had two in that deep hole. Shelter, even if it was a tumbling-down house, and attitude. She wouldn't have given up. Would two be enough to survive? I knew you could live for a while without food but not so long without water. And it had been so cold. How long had it been? Two or three days?

I was feeling muddled. And every now and then Kitty's face came into my mind, but I couldn't deal with thinking about her right now.

The large swinging door opened again, and the next person that came through I recognized. It was Grandma. She held a little plastic cup of tea, and she blew on it as she walked over and sat beside me.

"She's going to be all right, isn't she, Grandma?"

Grandma put an arm around me and gave me a squeeze. "Of course she is, Nate."

---

They wanted Mum to stay in the hospital overnight because she was very dehydrated. Her leg was broken and they'd put a big cast on it that went from her ankle to her knee. We could go and see her, but only for a little while because she was very, very tired.

When we walked into the room, Mum turned her head on her white pillow and she smiled.

I stopped by the door. I was feeling overwhelmed with everything, and I didn't want to cry so I dug my nails into my palms. Grandma put her tea down and went over and stroked Mum's forehead. They said something to each other but I couldn't hear what it was, and Grandma gave her a kiss. There was a bag of fluid hanging on a metal stand next to the bed, and the long tube snaked down and into her hand. Mum looked over at me, and I took a few steps closer.

"Oh, Nate. I'm so sorry . . ." she said, and she reached out for me, but I stayed where I was. I suddenly felt angry for everything she'd put me through. "I'm so sorry. You must have been so frightened not knowing what had happened."

I shrugged. "It's all right. I've been fine."

Grandma made noises about her tea not having any sugar in it, and then she headed to the door. I think she was just pretending about the sugar so that we could be alone. The door closed behind her with a *shush*.

"What happened, Mum?" I said. "What were you doing at the big house?"

Mum closed her eyes for a moment, then opened them again. "I went to the shop and got some food, and then as I was driving past the big old house, I suddenly wondered if there was any firewood around there that we could use. They'd forecast snow and I knew we needed to keep the wood stove going as that was the only heating we had."

I kept silent. Listening.

"I looked around outside, but there wasn't anything small enough or dry, so I went in to see if there were any old bits of furniture we could burn . . . and then I realized it wasn't safe. I was about to leave when . . . when the floor gave way . . ."

She closed her eyes and tears rolled down her cheeks. I reached out and held on to her hand.

"I couldn't move. My leg . . . My leg hurt so much and I couldn't get out. The doctor said it was lucky I was wearing a thick coat. And that you came, Nate. Another day without water and . . ."

I squeezed her hand tightly, and she looked up at me.

"What did you do, Nate? You must have been so worried. Did you find anything to eat?"

"Yes, there was loads in the cupboards. And I burnt all the wood we had and kept the place nice and warm."

"You did that? All on your own?"

I nodded.

"And the chicken laid some eggs, so I had them as well," I added.

Mum smiled. "It's your birthday too. I'm so sorry, Nate. I'll make it up to you, I promise."

I tried to say that it was fine and that my birthday had been fine, but I had a huge knot in my throat, so I just nodded again.

"I thought you'd gone back to him, Mum. I thought you'd left me to go back to Gary."

Her forehead creased as tears trickled down her cheeks. "Go back to him? Whatever made you think I'd do that? Oh, Nate. I didn't mean to leave you. And we're never going back to him. Okay? Never."

She stared at me and I stared at her, and then she mouthed the words:

*I love you.*

And I mouthed the same words back.

———————————

Grandma had booked us into a local hotel, and on the drive there I told her everything that had been going on at home with Gary. I even told her about the light bulbs. She didn't say much, but when we got to our room, she called my dad in America, who said he was leaving on the next available flight. She asked me if I wanted to speak to him, but I just shook my head.

Our room in the hotel had two beds, and that night Grandma lay next to me and asked me why Mum hadn't told her about Gary. I didn't know what to say, so I shut my eyes and pretended to be asleep.

I lay awake for hours worrying about Mum. What if she suddenly got worse in the night? What if something happened to her?

My head hurt remembering when the man in the orange jacket opened the door of the house. Of course no one lived there. How could I have been so stupid? The place was practically falling down. But what did that mean about Kitty? Who was she? Where had she come from?

I must have dozed off, but I was woken in the early morning when Grandma's cell phone began to ring. I rolled over. Grandma was dressed and sitting on her bed with her back to me. As she spoke to the person on the other end she rubbed her head and said "Okay" over and over. I stared at her back and felt sick. I couldn't tell if it was a bad phone call or a good phone call.

Grandma hung up and turned to me.

"That was the hospital," she said, and I felt a flood of relief as she smiled. "They said your mum is doing well, and she can go home later today."

I grinned back at her and then jumped out of bed to get dressed.

———————————

On the drive to the hospital Grandma kept asking if I was okay.

"I'm going to suggest to your mum that you both come back and live with me. For a while, at least. Does that sound like a good idea?"

My heart leapt. "That sounds like a great idea," I said and I gave her a big smile.

# CHAPTER 31

# GOING BACK TO THE COTTAGE

We drove straight from the hospital to the cottage, as we needed to pick up our things. The doctor had said that Mum needed to go for another X-ray on her leg and he talked about physical therapy, but we could do that at the hospital that was closer to Grandma's house.

Dad arrived just before we left. He was shaking a bit and he gave me a very long hug. He knew all about Gary because Grandma had told him on the phone. I told him it hadn't been true what I'd said about Gary being like a father to me and that I'd only said it to make him feel bad. He smiled and said he understood. On his way from the airport he'd checked out our house, but when he got there Gary was loading up his car.

Dad confronted him and Gary said he'd been planning to get away from us and "this stupid town" all along. He said it was a relief that Mum and I had left because now he was free to go on to bigger and better things. Dad laughed at him and started to say he was a coward and a bully, but Gary sped off before he could finish.

Dad was sure that would be the last we'd ever see of Gary. Dad was here for a whole two weeks, so he said he'd come and see me at Grandma's and I gave him an extra big hug when he said that.

We pulled up outside the cottage and Grandma gasped. "I can't believe you stayed here all on your own, Nate. How did you manage?"

I didn't think it actually looked that bad today. The sun was shining and there were even a few green shoots poking through the slushy snow, trying to hurry winter out of the way to make room for spring. Mum twisted around from the passenger seat.

"How're you doing?" she asked.

"I'm fine," I said. And I was.

"Right, let's go inside and get our things together, shall we?" she said, getting her crutches ready. Grandma began saying that Mum should wait in the car, but I think she realized that Mum wanted to go in, even if she had to take it slowly.

The kitchen door was still slightly ajar and I pushed it open. The washing-up bowl was still sitting beside the garbage can, but there was no sign of the chicken.

Being back in the cottage was really weird. Grandma started tutting about the state of the place, and Mum just looked like she wanted to sit down. I was hoping that there would be some sign of Sam—I had so many questions to ask him, but I didn't think it was likely.

Mum looked at me for a minute, checking if I was all right.

"We won't be long, okay?" she said, and I nodded.

Grandma picked up the parcel on the table that had been left in the empty coal bunker by the delivery man. She turned it over in her hands.

"Someone sent a parcel to William. I wonder who?" she said, squinting at the address. She began to rip the packet open.

"I think I'm going to go and have one last look around outside," I said. "I won't be long."

Mum looked worried, but I smiled so she could see I was all right and then headed out to the garden.

The birds were singing so loudly in the woods, it was like they'd all decided to get together and make a forest choir. I made my way through William's Gate, past the tire swing.

I could see Kitty in the distance.

She was standing by the same tree where I'd met her just a few days ago. Her brown satchel was over her shoulder, her hat was pulled down tightly on her head, and she had her shovel in her hand.

And then I saw her color.

She hadn't been freezing all those times before. Her lips weren't blue from the cold—that was her glow. I could see it clearly now. But Kitty's glow was like Arthur's; it was faded.

"Nate!" she said, a big grin across her face when she spotted me. "I'm so glad you're here! Are you back for good?"

She leaned on the shovel's handle, just like she had before.

"No, Kitty. I can't stay," I said, studying her closely. Her eyes were bright and shining.

Shrugging, she sighed deeply and scraped the shovel half-heartedly in the dirt. I took a step closer.

"So . . . you're . . . you're one of them?" I said.

She looked up at me, but she didn't say anything.

"You're . . . You're imaginary. Right?" I continued.

Her shoulders dropped and she nodded. "I was the *best* imaginary friend anyone could wish for. And I loved my friend dearly."

I smiled. "It was Charlotte, wasn't it? You were Charlotte's friend? That's why you were so determined to finish the treasure hunt."

Kitty nodded. "I miss her, Nate. I miss her so much."

She stared at the ground, her face sad.

"I've been on my own now for years. Many, many years."

She looked back up at me, hopeful.

"It was great though, wasn't it, Nate? Solving the treasure hunt together? I really enjoyed having a friend again." Her forehead relaxed a little.

"But why didn't you tell me who you were, Kitty? Why say you were James's daughter?"

She put her head to one side as she thought about it. "I think . . . It's been so long . . . I've been here for so long, all on my own, that maybe I forgot who I was. Do you think that's right?"

I opened my mouth and closed it again. I couldn't find the right words. She'd seemed so real to me; maybe that *is* what happened. That she had been here so long she'd forgotten she was imaginary.

I cleared my throat.

"I don't know. Maybe? I don't really know, Kitty," I said.

She sighed and her gentle blue glow faded a little. "And now you're leaving." Her pale eyes blinked at me.

"Yes. I have to go."

She dropped her head.

"But . . . But . . . Now that you've remembered who you are again, maybe you just need to find someone else who needs you," I said. "Someone else who needs a friend."

She looked puzzled for a moment, but I could see her blue eyes beginning to twinkle again. "Do you think?"

I nodded. "Yes! There must be hundreds of kids out there who need you. Thousands!"

Her color was slowly returning. "I guess so."

"And you're not going to find them in a deserted wood, are you?"

She thought about it and smiled, but then her face quickly fell again. "But I don't know how. I've forgotten how to, Nate."

I thought back to my birthday and when I was talking to Sam about Arthur. Everything he'd said came back to me.

"You've got to let go. You've got to let go of Charlotte. If you let go, then you are ready to find someone new!"

"Let go? Are you sure?" she said.

I nodded, grinning.

"Okay . . . I'm not sure how. I'm not sure how to . . ."

I watched as she closed her eyes and took a few breaths. She could see something in her mind, I was sure, and she was moving her lips.

"Goodbye," she whispered. So quietly I could hardly hear her. "Goodbye, Charlotte."

Her face widened into a broad smile, and as it did, a blue glow shone out of her like a brilliant light. I laughed and blinked as it dazzled my eyes.

"Ha! You're doing it, Kitty! You're really doing it!"

She opened her eyes for a second, the bright blue sparkling in front of me, and she opened her mouth to say something, but then she was gone. Her brilliant color faded away into the trees.

I stood there for a moment, getting my breath back from what I'd witnessed. Had that really just happened? I laughed and clutched my chest as I took some deep breaths. And then I sighed.

"Goodbye, Kitty," I said. "And thank you for being my friend."

----

When I got back to the cottage the front door was wide open and Grandma was just closing the trunk of the car.

"Right. We're all done. You ready, Nate?" said Mum from the passenger seat.

I looked up at the gray cottage, the dark ivy glinting in the sunlight.

"I just want to check I haven't left anything lying around. Is that okay?" I said.

Mum watched me for a moment, and then she nodded.

I went through the door and made my way upstairs. I tried not to think about it too much, but what I was really doing was looking out for a flash of yellow to see if Sam was still around.

But there was nothing.

The bedroom I'd slept in looked brighter now that the sun was shining. Grandma or Mum must have made the cowboy duvet bed, as it was back to being neat and tidy, just how it was when we'd arrived.

I glanced into the other bedroom where Mum had slept and then the bathroom and then slowly made my way back downstairs.

I looked around the living room one last time, willing Sam to appear. I wanted to tell him I was all right, that me and Mum were going to be okay.

I stood on the rug by the wood stove where I'd seen him last and I stared toward the corner where he'd disappeared. I stared and I stared and I stared, but there was just the dappled sunlight dancing against the wall.

I cleared my throat.

"Sam. If you're there, I want you to know I'm fine. I'm not sure if you can hear me, but we're . . . we're going to live at Grandma's. For a while, at least. Gary . . . Gary's moved a long, long way away and Mum is going to talk to someone about how he treated us. We might go back to our house at some point, but not just yet. I . . . I wanted you to know . . . I just wanted you to know I'm okay."

I cleared my throat, as I was sounding croaky.

"And can you . . . can you look out for a girl named Kitty? Maybe you knew she was imaginary, I don't know. Did you? Did you know and not tell me? Well anyway, if you do see her, can you tell her she has the most beautiful color?"

I wiped my eyes and turned to go.

As I passed the dining table I saw the parcel addressed to William that Grandma had opened earlier. Hiding with Sam behind the sofa while someone banged on the front door felt like a lifetime ago now.

I held the parcel in my hands, then carefully took out what was inside. It was a square, flat shape covered in bubble wrap and on the top was a letter. I began to read:

*Dear William,*

*I hope that this letter finds you well, and I'm so sorry for not keeping in touch with you all these years. As you know, after Charlotte died my family didn't feel they could continue to live in the house for long, so we moved away. We're now living in France, and I have five grandchildren. Can you believe it? Time goes so quickly, doesn't it?*

*I hope you've enjoyed your retirement, in your little cottage. I still think of the old, grand house from time to time and of the happy times I spent there with dear*

*Charlotte. We loved solving your ingenious treasure*
*hunts. Do you remember? It was such fun running*
*around the grounds, trying to work out the answers to*
*the clues.*

*I was sorting through some old family papers recently,*
*and I came across a photograph that I thought you would like*
*to have. I think you'll agree it is a wonderful picture; our*
*happiness certainly shines through.*

*Well, like I said at the start, I'm sorry for not keeping in*
*touch with you, dear William, and I hope this letter finds*
*you in good spirits. Take care, my friend.*

*Yours,*
*James Turner-Wright*

I put the letter on the table and carefully undid the bubble
wrap. Inside was a brown picture frame, and I carefully turned it
over. It was a photograph. In the middle was an old man wearing
green boots, brown trousers, and suspenders, and he had his shirt-
sleeves rolled up. On either side of him were two children.

"That must be William," I whispered to myself. "And that's
James when he was a boy. And that must be Charlotte."

The girl in the photo held a large, folded piece of paper in her
hand, and I could just make out something on the front in tiny
writing: *Treasure Map*. It looked like they were about to set off on an
adventure. James had his arms folded, and he was grinning straight

at the camera. Charlotte was laughing too, but she wasn't looking at the camera. She was looking to one side.

At first I wondered if somebody I couldn't see behind the camera was making her laugh, but then I spotted it. There was a haze beside her. A bluish kind of haze. And Charlotte was looking straight at it and smiling.

"Oh my . . ." I whispered to myself.

I traced the blue glow with my finger.

"Kitty," I whispered. I wiped the glass frame with my sleeve and then I smiled. "I see you, Kitty. I can see you there," I said, as if she could hear me.

I took the frame and went to the mantelpiece and pushed some of the ornaments to one side. I placed the framed photograph of William, James, and Charlotte in the center, and their smiles beamed out over the living room.

"All set, Nate?" said Grandma, poking her head around the front door. "I need to lock up now."

I took one last look around the room.

"All set, Grandma," I said.

I picked up my backpack with my light jar safely tucked inside, and then I headed out to my family in the car.

# About the Author

Lisa Thompson is the author of *The Goldfish Boy, The Light Jar,* and *The Day I Was Erased.* She has worked as a radio broadcast assistant—first at the BBC and then for an independent production company—making plays and comedy programs. During this time, she got to make tea for lots of famous people. She lives in Suffolk, England, with her family. Find her at lisathompsonauthor.com and on Twitter at @lthompsonwrites.

Keep reading for a sneak peek at Lisa Thompson's
*The Day I Was Erased*!

# CHAPTER 1

# GARBAGE

My dog, Monster, is the best in the world: FACT.

Dad says he's probably half dog, half mole because he's so good at digging tunnels: mainly underneath our garden fence. He's really round, so it's a miracle he doesn't get stuck.

I watched him do it once. He sat on the flower bed and stared at the wooden panels, as if he was trying to work out how to tackle them, and then he began to dig. Dirt flew from under his wagging tail, and then he did this weird shuffling-along-on-his-stomach thing with his back legs flattened on either side. The next second he was gone.

When he escapes, he always heads to the same place: Mrs. Banks's front garden. He charges at her garbage cans, knocks them over, and then, like a big, furry vacuum cleaner, gobbles everything up. And I mean *everything*. He threw up a pair of underwear onto the living room carpet once, and Mum wasn't sure if she should wash them and take them back to Mrs. Banks. I pointed out that if they were in the garbage in the first place, then she obviously didn't want them, did she?

Mrs. Banks caught Monster going through her garbage for the third time this week. She arrived on our doorstep with him tucked backward under her arm. His tail was wagging around and around, like it does when he's happy, and she had to put her head to one side to stop it from hitting her in the face.

"You do realize that this animal is completely out of control, don't you, Mrs. Beckett?" she said. Mum was a bit flustered because she'd been in the middle of an argument with Dad when she answered the door. Monster stopped wagging and began to wriggle, but the more he wriggled the more Mrs. Banks gripped on to him.

"He's been going through my trash again. *And* he left a 'present' on my lawn."

"A present?" said Mum, rubbing her forehead.

"Yes, Mrs. Beckett. A present. The foul, smelly, disgusting kind."

Monster's tail wagged again as if he were showing us all where the "present" had come from. I snorted and Mrs. Banks shot a look at me. There was a high-pitched yelp as she tightened her grip around my dog even more.

"You shouldn't be holding him like that!" I shouted. "He doesn't like it. You let him go right now, you mean old . . . cow!"

"Maxwell!" said Mum.

Mrs. Banks's eyes went so wide I thought they were going to fall out of her head.

"Are you going to let your son . . . your *child* talk to me in that way?"

Mum looked at me and opened her mouth, but nothing came out. It was as if she didn't have a clue what to say. Monster's tail had stopped wagging now and he began to whine. I jumped off our step and tried to grapple him out of Mrs. Banks's arms.

"You're hurting him! Let go of him! Let go of him now!"

Mrs. Banks let out a squeal. "Oh! Get off! Get off me, you . . . you horror!"

"Maxwell! What has come over you?" cried Mum, pulling me

back by my shoulder. Monster dropped to the ground with a yelp. He gave himself a quick shake, then trotted inside as if nothing had happened.

"I'm so sorry, Mrs. Banks. Maxwell isn't usually like this."

Mrs. Banks swept her hair out of her face.

"I beg to differ, Mrs. Beckett. Your son is a beast. I know it, the school knows it, and I'm pretty sure *you* know it. I suggest you get that dog *and your son* under control, or I'll inform the authorities."

She turned on her heel and stormed off down the pathway and through the space in the wall where the gate used to be. Mum closed the door, taking a deep breath. I knew she was about to have a go at me, but Dad started yelling from the kitchen.

"Amanda?! Have you been eating my chicken pasta? Taking the Post-it off doesn't mean it's yours!"

Mum gritted her teeth, then stomped down the hallway.

"No, Eddie! I haven't touched your flipping pasta!"

I huffed. My parents had this stupid arrangement where they each bought their own food and put Post-its on what was theirs. If they thought the other one had eaten something that didn't belong to them, they went nuts. My sister, Bex, and I didn't use labels; we just ate whatever Mum or Dad cooked for us. I hated those Post-its. I hated them nearly as much as I hated Mrs. Banks for hurting my dog.

———

Mum and Dad had a massive fight that night. One of their worst. I was trying to go to sleep, but I could hear them through the bedroom wall shouting at each other.

I wanted to go into Bex's room and sit it out with her, like we used to do during a thunderstorm when we were little. Bex would never let me in her room now, though. She's fifteen and a total nerd. She's even got a poster on her wall with the names of all the kings and queens of England on it. I mean, who does that? Why doesn't she have a pop group or a film star or something a *normal* fifteen-year-old girl would have? Still, I'd rather have been in her room than on my own listening to them argue.

Mum and Dad shouted about Monster and Mrs. Banks and then turned to me. They were blaming each other for all the trouble I kept getting into at school. I wrapped my pillow around my head and tried to doze off until finally, at about midnight, I heard the front door slam. I sat up and listened as Dad's van started and sped off down the road. I relaxed a bit then. Dad just drives around until he's calmed down, and he comes home when we're all asleep.

I pulled the blanket over my head and curled up into a ball. If Mrs. Banks hadn't knocked with Monster under her arm, then there wouldn't have been all that shouting. It was all Mrs. Banks's fault. As I drifted off to sleep, I thought of a way to get my revenge.

# CHAPTER 2
# FLAMINGO

The pink flamingo on Mrs. Banks's lawn was looking at me funny. Its black, staring eye didn't move as I crouched down in the corner of the garden.

I walked past Mrs. Banks's house every day on my way to and from school. She lives next door to my friend Reg, and the tall plastic flamingo had appeared beside her pond about a month ago. Mrs. Banks was in her garden most days, admiring the flamingo or moving it into a slightly different position. I wouldn't be surprised if she actually talked to it. Well, that stupid bird was going to get it.

A prickly bush beside me began to shake, and a wet nose emerged from the undergrowth and sniffed the air.

"Monster! How did you get out again? Keep down. She'll skin you alive if she gets ahold of you, you do know that, don't you?" Monster head-butted me on my side and I rubbed his neck. His bottom wiggled madly as his tail propelled itself around and around.

I stared back at the flamingo and held on to a half piece of brick I'd found in our back garden.

"Who would buy something so ugly, Monster? That flamingo is the most disgusting thing I've ever seen." He licked the back of my hand and I wiped the stringy, sticky goo onto my school trousers. "In fact, the whole garden is hideous," I said. "Look at it!"

There were stepping stones from the front gate to the door so there was no risk that any visitor would walk on her precious grass. Not that I'd ever known her to have visitors. No one called at Mrs. Banks's house for a cup of tea or to see how she was doing. However, plenty of people stopped as they walked by to gawk at the garden. Not because it was beautiful or full of tropical plants or anything, but because it was so . . . *cheesy*. Dotted among the bright-colored flowers were a family of concrete squirrels wearing top hats, seven pixies in various gymnastic poses, an old man with a big fat tummy pushing a tiny wheelbarrow, and a plastic wishing well. The pink flamingo was her latest purchase, and only this morning I'd watched her wipe some invisible dirt off it as I walked to school. It was clearly her new favorite thing.

I held tightly on to the brick and looked at the windows of Mrs. Banks's bungalow. She had blinds in her windows like the ones you get in offices—the vertical kind, in a horrible, dirty green color. They were all closed.

"Right. Are you ready for this?" I said. Monster did a deep sigh next to me, then began to lick his butt. He always does that when he gets bored.

"Okay," I said as I stood up. "Three, two, one . . ." I twisted the brick around in my hand, then took a shot . . .

Now, what I'd intended to do was quite different from what actually happened. What I'd *intended* to do was to knock the bird over and maybe give it a bit of a dent in its stupid plastic head. It might not sound like much, but for Mrs. Banks, finding her brand-new flamingo lying on her perfect lawn would have been enough to send her into a total meltdown.

But what actually happened was this:

The piece of brick flew out of my hand and spun around as it hurtled toward the bacon-pink bird. I watched with my mouth open as I waited for it to reach its target. And reach it, it most certainly did. It not only hit the flamingo, it took its head clean off with one almighty CRACK!

The plastic head somersaulted into the air and landed on Mrs. Banks's doorstep like some sick parcel delivery. The decapitated body stayed exactly where it was, its skinny legs still rooted into the ground.

"Oops," I whispered. I slowly backed away toward the low fence. The vertical blinds began to twitch.

"Come on, Monster. We'd better run," I said. I grabbed my school bag and clambered over the fence while my dog tried to squeeze through a tiny gap. He'd managed to get in that way, but now he was struggling to fit through. He was stuck.

"Pull yourself, Monster!" I said as he just stood there, wagging his tail at me. "We've gotta go!"

I was about to jump back over the fence and push his rear through when he did one more strain and burst out onto the pavement. He gave himself a shake, then looked up at me as if to say, "Right. What next?"

I began to laugh as we ran. A headless flamingo! Right there in her garden! It couldn't have gone better. She would probably explode from anger. She'd open her front door, see the head lying there on her doormat, and erupt like a fiery volcano. We turned the corner and slowed to a walk as we got closer to home.

"We'd better keep our heads down for a bit now. Just in case she suspects. She's going to be *so* mad," I said.

I turned up our garden path and let myself in, throwing my bag on the stairs and kicking the door shut behind me. Monster trotted off to the kitchen to check if anything had appeared in his food bowl.

"Mum? The printer's run out of ink and I need to get my project . . . Oh, it's you." My sister, Bex, appeared at the top of the stairs. She crossed her arms. "Have you been in a fight again? Mum'll go mad."

I looked down at my school uniform. My shirt was hanging out of my trousers and ripped at the side where I'd caught it on Mrs. Banks's fence. My shoes were brown from mud, rather than the regulation black, and my tie was wrapped around my left wrist. I hated wearing a tie. All in all, I looked pretty normal.

"You do know you'll be grounded again, don't you?" said Bex, stomping down the stairs and pushing past me.

"I haven't been in a fight," I said, following her to the kitchen. "I've actually been very busy teaching Mrs. Banks a lesson."

Bex ignored me and began rummaging through the kitchen drawers.

Mum and Dad were both out, so the house was quiet for once. I opened the fridge and tutted when I saw the fluttering of yellow Post-its. There was one with a name written on it attached to nearly every item of food or drink. Some said *Amanda* and some said *Eddie*. On a bottle of white wine there was one Post-it that read: *Amanda's. DO NOT TOUCH THIS UNDER ANY CIRCUMSTANCES.*

I took a bottle of Coke that didn't have a Post-it on it, which meant Bex or I could have it.

"Why don't they just have two fridges? Surely that would be better than all those stupid labels," I said, slamming the door.

"Maxwell, do you have *any* idea where the printer ink cartridges are? I need some urgently," said Bex, opening another drawer.

I took a big swig of Coke. "Oh yeah! I do, actually," I said.

Bex turned to me. "Fantastic! Where are they?"

I took another gulp, held up my hand, and then:

"YURRRPPPP."

I let out the loudest belch I could. Bex huffed.

"You are a disgusting human being. Do you realize that, Maxwell Beckett?"

I laughed as I took a bag of chips out of the cupboard. I pulled off the Post-it that said *Eddie* on the front and stuffed it into the garbage. Dad wouldn't mind me eating his chips. It was only when Mum ate them that he had a meltdown. I shoved a handful into my mouth as Bex searched through a cupboard.

"Are there any in your room?" she said. "*Please*, Maxwell. I want to print my Persian Empire project."

I didn't even know what that was, but I was pretty sure it was something she had done "for fun" rather than for homework. Like I said before, my sister is weird.

I pretended to think about where the ink cartridges could possibly be by putting my head to one side and tapping my chin with my finger.

"Let me see . . . I think they might be . . . um . . . No. No idea, I'm afraid," I said, showing her a mouthful of mashed-up chips.

Bex groaned and turned away.

"Urgh, you're so disgusting," she said. "Why were you even born?"

I grinned to myself, then balled up the chip bag and threw it in the trash.